THE BARON AND
THE UNFINISHED PORTRAIT

She heard a man say : 'Good morning.
Mrs. John Mannering ?'
'Yes,' Josephine said. She would add : 'Who
shall I say wishes to see her ?' and would then
make an effort to recollect whether the loft-
ladder was up or down ; if up, then 'Mrs.
Mannering' was out.
But those words did not come. Instead, Lorna
heard a peculiar gasp, followed by silence.
Lorna leaned forward, listening intently. There
was a heavy thump and the loud slamming of
the front door.

D1514019

Also by the same author

Affair for the Baron
The Baron in France
Salute for the Baron
Danger for the Baron
Nest Egg for the Baron
The Baron and the Missing Old Masters
The Baron Goes East
Frame the Baron

and available in Coronet Books

The Baron and the Unfinished Portrait

John Creasey
as
Anthony Morton

CORONET BOOKS
Hodder Paperbacks Ltd., London

Copyright © 1969 by John Creasey
First printed 1969 by Hodder & Stoughton Ltd
Coronet edition 1972

The characters in this book are entirely imaginary and
bear no relation to any living person.

This book is sold subject to the condition that it shall
not, by way of trade or otherwise, be lent, re-sold,
hired out or otherwise circulated without the publisher's
prior consent in any form of binding or cover other
than that in which this is published and without a similar
condition including this condition being imposed on the
subsequent purchaser.

Printed in Great Britain
for Coronet Books, Hodder Paperbacks Ltd.,
St. Paul's House, Warwick Lane, London, E.C.4,
by Richard Clay (The Chaucer Press), Ltd.,
Bungay, Suffolk.

ISBN 0 340 16210 4

CONTENTS

CHAPTER 1

A STORM IN A TEACUP

JOHN MANNERING sat in a winged armchair in his flat in an old house in Green Street, Chelsea. If he turned his head towards the right he saw the pageant of London's river on a lovely summer evening, small craft abounding, lighters and barges moving sluggishly through the still water, pleasure boats crowded with people passing to and fro. Between him and the river were plane trees in full leaf, but not yet dark green, for it was June. If he turned his head towards the left, he had another, very different picture.

Of his wife.

She was intent on some photographic prints, spread out on a low table. She looked puzzled and preoccupied, and now and again she frowned. His perspective of her heightened the breadth of her forehead, rendering the whole face heart-shaped. Her dark hair, with a few strands of grey, was drawn straight back, but fell, like wings, over her temples. Her dark lashes seemed to be swept upward from her clear grey eyes.

She glanced at him, realising that he had been looking at her. For a moment her gaze was straight, almost sombre; in such moments she could look sullen. Suddenly, her lips parted and she threw her head back. The movement, feminine, provocative, gave her an added attraction.

Mannering stared at her for a long time before saying: 'Like a drink?'

'I don't think so,' she said.

'Like any help?'

'No,' she said positively. 'This is something I need to work out for myself.'

'So you want to be alone,' he said.

'I want to put these away and forget them until the morning,' she replied.

'That's what I hoped to hear,' he said. Quite suddenly he was on his feet and standing beside her, and she was holding out her hands . . .

Later, when it was dark, she lay asleep and he awake.

He was remembering the time, not very long ago, when they had been drifting apart, and it had seemed as if nothing could hold them together. To this day he was not quite sure what had in fact held them, but such nights as this held a greater tenderness, a greater sense of fulfilment, than they had known in the days when their love had been more passionate.

He could hear her soft, even breathing, and could make out the shape of her cheek and forehead against the pillow. The sweep of her eyelashes reminded him of the way she had looked from his chair in the window. She had been so preoccupied about the photographs, but had left them spread out on the table without further thought. He smiled with near laughter.

A gust of wind shook the window and the curtain billowed into the room. Far off, there was a rumble of thunder. So there was a break in the weather, and the possibility of heavy rain. The sensible thing was to close the window, or at least push it to. That would mean getting up and he did not want to. He was snug and lazy, and if he got up he would go back to his own room and the spell would be broken. He dozed—and was startled by a vivid flash, then by a crack of thunder directly overhead. He realised that he must have been asleep, no storm would move so fast. Then he heard the sharp impact of rain against the window and had no choice but to get up.

Had he secured the window in the sitting-room?

Pushing the bedclothes back stealthily, anxious not to disturb Lorna, he half-grimaced, half-grinned. He hadn't secured windows or doors or anything at all!

As he closed the bedroom window, a fork of lightning split the sky and lit up the squat towers of the Battersea Power Station and the mass of foliage across the river. For a stupefying moment the Thames was a mirror reflecting the savage streaks of light. Darkness fell with opaque completeness: then another crack of thunder came directly above the house.

'John!' gasped Lorna. '*John!*'

He swung round and saw her starting up in bed, frightened yet now knowing what had wakened her. Another streak of lightning showed her face vividly, hands stretched out for reassurance, shoulders smooth and glowing as marble. He went across to her quickly, and put his arms round her.

'We've incurred the wrath of the gods,' he said lightly.

'How long has it been going on?'

'On and off for quite a time,' he told her. 'But the rain has only just started. I was going to shut the window in the sitting-room.'

'Is this one open at all?'

'Just a crack at the top.'

'I don't like the windows closed when there's lightning about,' Lorna remarked.

'I won't close it completely,' he promised.

Another savage flash, another terrifying crack, came before he reached the door. Lorna was pulling the bedclothes up to her neck and looking towards the window. Mannering crossed the small landing and felt a gust of wind; a door slammed. He went into the sitting-room to find the curtain billowing, the photographs scattered over the floor, a newspaper blowing about and rustling in one corner. As he neared the window, rain spattered coldly on his face. He closed the window with a bang, and stood back. This view showed an even longer stretch of the river, and a lightning fork seemed to turn the surface to molten gold.

He collected the photographs, one of which felt damp. He put on a light and looked down at the face of a woman.

She was quite remarkably beautiful.

He knew her slightly, having met her at various social functions both before and after her marriage. She was a Mrs. Cornelius Vandemeyer, young wife of a man of great wealth and culture, a renowned collector of *objets d'art* and one of the better customers at Mannering's Mayfair shop.

Why had Lorna been so intent on these photographs?

He took them into the bedroom with him, flicking on the switch of a subdued light.

The storm now seemed farther away, much less of a threat. He took a paper handkerchief from a box on the dressing-table, and dabbed the photograph before putting it on the dressing-table with the others.

'No damage done,' he reported cheerfully.

'It's a good thing you thought of the window, the carpet would have been ruined,' Lorna remarked. 'It's getting quieter, isn't it?'

'Yes,' said Mannering. 'Feel bold enough to stay on your own?'

'If the storm comes back again, I shall come rushing in to you!'

Mannering brushed her forehead with his lips and turned away; he was at the door before she asked: 'Do you know Deirdre Vandemeyer well?'

'Nothing like so well as I know her husband. Why?'

'I—oh, it doesn't matter,' Lorna said, with sudden impatience. 'Just a silly idea. I started a portrait of her a few months ago, and went to see her again yesterday, to discuss finishing it.'

'And wasn't she keen?'

'What on earth made you ask that?' demanded Lorna.

'You weren't very happy when you were studying the photographs,' Mannering pointed out.

'So there must be a problem!' Lorna frowned. 'It's impossible to repress the great detective in you, isn't it? Let's talk about it in the morning.'

'Of course. Sleep well,' Mannering said, and closed the door.

The sheets in his own bed were chilly, and made him even more wide awake. He lay looking at the distant lightning, his thoughts still with his wife. Tonight had brought them closer than they had been for a long time, yet the phrase she had used: 'It's impossible to repress the great detective in you, isn't it?' had been uttered with real feeling—the kind of feeling which had once been like a thickening wedge between them.

The 'great detective'!

He tried to put the thought out of his mind but it would not go, and he got up suddenly and went into the sitting-room. Inside an Elizabethan settle, carved with knights in armour, were several press-cutting books. He took them out and put them on the table where the photographs had been, and began to turn the pages.

There were headlines and articles about big jewel robberies carried out with great daring and skill, and intermixed with these stories were others about 'The Baron'. '*Jewel thief extraordinary*', the newspapers called him '*Raffles in Real Life*'. '*The Robin Hood of Crime*'. Feature articles followed fast upon one another, of the Baron who stole from the unjust rich and gave to the deserving poor.

It was a past age. There would be no scope in Britain for such a man today. How a few decades could change society! And how they had changed him——

Had they changed him enough? he wondered.

Lorna, at heart, did not think so. That was the crux of all their differences.

Yet in the very early days, embittered and vengeful towards society, he *had* robbed for personal gain. It had been Lorna who had swung him from that, and largely because of her he had become a kind of Robin Hood. How absurdly melodramatic the soubriquet seemed to him now!

He had bought Quinns, and with Lorna's eager approval turned it into one of the most famous shops in the world for jewellery and antiques. Since then he had never stolen—but he had, as a private investigator, often forced entry and broken safes, for the benefit of clients who had good reason not to work through the law. And as the years had passed, not only had the conflict between the Baron and Scotland Yard, then represented by Chief Superintendent William Bristow, ceased, but he was even, on occasions, consulted by them.

Yet Lorna, he knew, wanted him to stop all his activities except buying and selling and acting as a consultant.

Could he blame her?

Whether or no he could blame her—could he ever stop?

At heart he knew that it would be almost impossible, and that even if he tried he would soon fall from grace.

The issue had been forced between them several times but had not been raised for nearly a year. Perhaps he was wrong in thinking that it had been raised tonight.

Tired, woken in fright, all her emotions had been near the surface and she had spoken without thinking, reflecting a strongly held, though usually unvoiced opinion. Was it always the same with a married couple? Was there always some conflict between them, buried or outweighed at times by the strength of love but always latent, always liable to flare up when it was least expected?

With a sigh, he closed the books and put them away. There was no light under Lorna's door, so she was presumably asleep. All was quiet now, even the hissing and spatting of the rain had stopped, and the sky was star-lit, the river dark but calm.

He got into bed and was asleep within five minutes.

When he woke, Lorna was looking down on him, smiling, holding a tea-tray. She looked rested and attractive and Mannering's half-formed fears of the night were blown away. She put the tray on the bedside table, kissed him lightly on the cheek, took newspapers from under her arm and spread them over him.

'There's news for you,' she announced lightly.

There was something on her mind. It showed in her eyes. Mannering sat up and scanned the front page of *The Times*—and saw a small paragraph with the headline: *'Scotland Yard Chief Retires'*. Lorna poured out and Mannering read on:

'Chief Superintendent William Bristow, Scotland Yard's expert on jewels, is to retire at the end of

August—just thirty-five years after he first joined the Metropolitan Police Force.'

'Tea, my love,' remarked Lorna, sweetly.

'I need something,' said Mannering, and then took the bull by the horns. 'I wonder if his wife put him up to this.'

'I shouldn't think she would need to,' replied Lorna. 'Most men come to their senses sooner or later!' She laughed easily, her expression innocent of reproach. 'We could ask them to dinner, and find out.'

'Yes, fix it,' approved Mannering, sipping his tea. 'Thirty-five years. My, my! I've known him for over twenty. He was only a boy when I first met him!'

'He isn't a boy now,' Lorna said drily.

'No, dear.' Mannering finished his tea as he scanned the main headline. 'No major disasters or political up-roars, I see. That makes a nice change!' He glanced at the bedside clock. 'After eight, I shouldn't be too long. I'm seeing Rennie at the shop at half-past nine. Will you be out, or up in the studio?'

'In, most of the day,' Lorna answered. He had the impression that she wanted to add something, but she stopped herself. 'I'll get breakfast while you have your bath.'

She went out—graceful and nearly as slim-waisted as she had been in those early days.

Mannering shaved while his bath-water ran, pondering over Rennie, a highly reputable dealer who did a lot of business with Quinns in Boston. There were three shops, now, the third in Paris, and Rennie was not in London as much as he had been at one time. Rennie, he suspected, was interested in a partnership, and Mannering wasn't sure that would be a good thing. If the Bostonian made a formal proposal, he would talk it over with Lorna before making a decision.

He went into the kitchen-cum-breakfast-room. The only help they had in the house, these days, was a daily who arrived at half-past nine; they had grown used to having the flat to themselves in the morning, and now very much preferred it. Eggs and bacon with fried bread and grilled tomatoes were on the hot-plate above the gas stove, and coffee was bubbling in a percolator. Lorna was reading a letter. Several letters were by Mannering's place. He opened them; all were pleasant, none was important. When he looked up, Lorna was staring at him intently, her letter still in her hand.

'John,' she said, 'promise not to crow.'

'Do I usually make such unpleasant noises?' he inquired lightly.

'Occasionally, if the opportunity arises,' she said wryly.

'And has it?'

'That's for you to decide,' replied Lorna. 'I want you to solve a problem for me. *I've* an instinctive feeling that something's wrong.'

He looked at her intently, and saw that she was serious. It dawned on him how much it must have cost her to confess to such an idea.

He gave a delighted smile, covered her free hand with his, and said with complete assurance:

'Lady Vandemeyer won't have her portrait finished, and you want to know the reason why. Is that it?'

'That's half of it,' said Lorna. 'She won't have it finished. But I think I know the reason why. I don't think she *is* Lady Vandemeyer.'

CHAPTER 2

A DELICATE MATTER

AFTER a long pause, Mannering said:

'You can't be serious.'

'You can't be awake,' Lorna retorted, 'or you'd know I am.'

'You mean——' Mannering paused, and then went on: 'You don't think Lady Vandemeyer *is* Lady Vandemeyer.'

'No, I don't,' Lorna reiterated simply.

Mannering frowned.

'We need to think and talk about this,' he said heavily.

'But if you're late already——'

'Rennie can wait for a while if he has to,' said Mannering. He helped himself to bacon and eggs while Lorna poured out coffee, and went on. 'When did this possibility occur to you?' When Lorna didn't reply immediately he continued very thoughtfully: 'There can't be many richer people in the world than Cornelius Vandemeyer.'

Lorna leaned forward. 'John, I started the portrait for the Cobe collection, they wanted a portrait by me and they also wanted Deirdre Vandemeyer. She was agreeable. I had to go to her, she wouldn't come here, but that wasn't unusual. You were abroad, I forget where, and the early stages didn't take very long. Then she became ill.'

'Ill,' Mannering echoed.

'Oh, nothing specific with a name,' said Lorna. 'I only know that I went there one morning about a month ago, and was told that Lady Vandemeyer wasn't well, but would let me know when she was ready for another sitting. I waited a week and then telephoned, and was given practically the same message.'

'After that you decided it was her turn to call you if she wanted the portrait finished?'

Lorna nodded.

'And she didn't call?'

'No,' said Lorna, 'but the Cobe Collection did.'

'Wanting the portrait?'

'Yes,' said Lorna. 'For their summer exhibition.'

'Had they paid anything?'

Lorna shook her head.

'So they weren't simply after their money's worth,' reasoned Mannering.

'Oh no, that wasn't it. They really wanted the portrait, and when I told them what had happened they said they would get in touch with Deirdre.'

'And did they?'

'I suppose they must have done. They rang me a little later to say she wouldn't be able to sit for a while, and asked me if I would wait until she could. And they offered to pay me in advance. As far as I was concerned there was nothing more to do except wait.'

'Well?' asked Mannering puzzled. 'What's worrying you?'

'I saw Deirdre at Harrods yesterday,' Lorna told him. 'An assistant was trying to sell her some Brussels lace, and called her Lady Vandemeyer. I looked round, went towards her and said how glad I was that she was better, and could soon begin to sit again. She was very charming and thanked me nicely, and said she hoped so—but I don't think she had the faintest idea who I was. So last night I got the photographs out and studied them. I'd taken them before starting the portrait, you know how much that helps me if there isn't a lot of time for sittings.' Mannering nodded. 'The more I looked the more sure I felt she wasn't the woman I'd met in Harrods.' Lorna got up for more coffee, then began to walk about the room with the percolator in her hand. 'I nearly told you about it then, but I wasn't sure you'd take me seriously.'

'Of course I take you seriously. But——'

'But you think she could have changed after the illness,' Lorna said drily.

'Well, couldn't she?'

'It's not that sort of change,' said Lorna. 'She didn't look paler, or thinner, in fact she looked in glowing health.' Lorna stopped by Mannering's side and refilled his cup. 'The eyes, too, were different—an opaque, china blue; far less translucent than the eyes of the woman I am painting. *They* can't have changed. And this one looked younger. In your wildest moments, what would you think, darling?'

'I think *you* think Deirdre Vandemeyer is being impersonated,' Mannering said.

'Yes, I do. I don't want to, but I do.'

'Is her husband in London, do you know?'

'Yes—he was at Sotheby's on Monday, remember.'

'I'd forgotten,' answered Mannering, 'but I remember now. I don't supose——' he broke off.

'Go on,' said Lorna. 'Speculate aloud.'

'Well, he couldn't possibly be fooled, could he?'

'By a substitute wife, do you mean?'

Mannering nodded.

'Hardly,' said Lorna, laughing. 'It sounds too absurd, doesn't it. Do you think I could have imagined the whole thing?'

'I suppose you *could* have been wrong. But I rather

hope you weren't!' There was a glint of humour in
Mannering's hazel eyes. 'Just the kind of thing I'd like to
work on! May I, darling?'

Lorna nodded. 'Yes, please.'

'It shall be done.'

'John——'

'No conditions,' Mannering interrupted firmly.

'Just one. That you tell me what you find out, and
don't spare my feelings if I've made a fool of myself.'

'I'll keep you up to date,' Mannering promised. 'Provided you haven't kept anything back, that is. I don't
want to start with half a story.'

'I really have told you everything I can,' Lorna assured
him.

'If you remember anything else let me know, won't
you?' said Mannering. 'You would be surprised how the
teeniest, weeniest clue, even a hunch——'

She laughed, quite gaily.

She was still laughing when he left the flat at twenty-
past nine, and she telephoned Quinns in Hart Row,
Mayfair, to let Rennie know that Mannering would be
late.

Mannering had parked his car outside the previous
night; his garage was one of several which had recently
been demolished to make a site for a block of flats, and he
was looking for another within easy walking distance. He
was driving a Jaguar, silver grey in colour, soft and silent
in movement. The storm had pocked the paint-work and
glass with grey rings, and he wiped the windscreen
briskly before getting in. As he closed the door a woman
entered the street from the King's Road end, and he
recognised Josephine, their daily. When she had first
come to work for Lorna, Mannering had asked her for

her full name, and she had said primly:

'Just Josephine.'

And Josephine she remained.

She was a well-preserved woman of middle-age, who dyed her hair to its original blackness, had a good complexion and nicely defined features. Always very punctilious, she stopped by the car.

'Good morning, sir.'

'Good morning, Josephine!'

Convention honoured, Josephine went along to the house. Once inside, she would, Mannering knew, indulging both a small vanity and an austere parsimony at the same time, don one of Lorna's discarded studio smocks, and work in it all day.

Mannering turned the corner into a stream of traffic, wrinkled his nose as a cloud of smoke billowed from the exhaust of a milk tanker in front of him, then glided ahead. It would take from fifteen to thirty minutes to reach Quinns, according to the density of the traffic.

He was there at a quarter to ten.

Quinns of London was a narrow-fronted shop in a narrow street, a relic of Elizabethan London. Opposite was an exclusive milliners, nearby an exclusive beauty salon—in Hart Lane every business had to be exclusive or it could not afford to be expensive. As he pulled up, the shop door opened and a young man appeared, particularly young for Quinns, Lionel Spencer. He was elegant and yet he looked durable; in fact, he was accomplished in judo and karate.

'Good morning, sir.' He opened the door.

'Good morning. Has Mr. Rennie been waiting long?'

'He telephoned to say he would be late,' said Lionel. 'So you need not have hurried. Shall I park the car for you, sir?'

It would have been cruel to say 'no'.

How different would things have been, Mannering wondered later, if he had stayed with Lorna for another half-hour?

The first thing Mannering did was to look through the post in his small, exquisitely furnished office at the back of Quinns. There was nothing of importance, nothing at all that was urgent. Larraby, his manager, was in the long, narrow shop and, with two junior assistants, was at the never-ending task of polishing and dusting, washing and cleaning, the countless precious things in stock. These varied from a jewel-encrusted Italian ring said to have belonged to Leonardo da Vinci, to a stool filched from the tomb of an early Egyptian king. Laying aside the last envelope, Mannering picked up the telephone and dialled New Scotland Yard. Almost at once a girl's voice intoned curtly:

'Scotland Yard . . . Help you?'

'Mr. Bristow, please.'

'Superintendent Bristow?'

'I didn't know there *was* any other Bristow at the Yard,' Mannering said, mildly.

'Oh, there are *several*,' the girl said loftily. 'You're through.'

A man who was not Bristow answered almost at once; another voice new to Mannering. It was over six months since he had called the Yard, and there had been many changes since the Metropolitan Police had moved into the new headquarters.

'Mr. Bristow's office,' the man said.

'Ask Mr. Bristow if he's free to take a call from John Mannering,' Mannering said.

'Mr. Mannering of Quinns, sir?'

'Yes.'

'I'm sure he would like to speak to you, sir. Just one moment.'

One moment grew into several until at last a familiar voice, enlivened by what sounded like genuine heartiness, came through.

'Hallo, John! I was only thinking of you yesterday.'

'I was only reading about you today,' retorted Mannering.

'Oh! Which particular newspaper?'

'*The Times.*'

'Ah, well, we all come to it. I've been teetering on the edge of retirement for some time, you know, and finally took the plunge.'

After a pause, Mannering said: 'Bill, it won't seem the same.'

'It won't be the same,' Bristow said gruffly. 'I shall miss it like hell.'

'Of course you will. Bill, remember one thing, will you?'

'Yes?'

'The Yard will miss you, too.'

'Oh, nonsense!' Bristow said bluffly. 'And let's get to business, John! What can I do for you?'

'I didn't ring on business,' Mannering said.

'You mean——' Bristow paused. 'You just rang for——' He could not find the right words.

'Old time's sake,' Mannering said lightly. 'Lorna is going to get in touch, soon, about dinner. Try to make it, won't you?'

'Be absolutely sure I will,' promised Bristow. 'Nice of you to call, John, I—well, very nice of you to call. I'll be seeing you.'

Mannering rang off slowly. He needed no telling that

Bristow was feeling sentimental, and very far from relish-
ing the thought of retirement. It flashed through his
mind that Larraby was also nearing retirement and could
not last much longer doing a full day's work—he was in
his middle seventies. Whereas Bristow ... Mannering
stifled the thought, giving a fierce little grin. Bristow, his
old enemy, manager of Quinns! *Now* who was feeling
sentimental?

Yet the idea that Bristow could be invaluable here,
kept returning.

Lorna was in her attic studio, approached from the
main flat by a loft-ladder which she could draw up whenever she wanted to be undisturbed. Two easels were
placed prominently. On one rested the unfinished portrait of Deirdre Vandemeyer; on the other were pinned
the photographs.

Propped casually against the walls were canvases in
various stages of completion. On the walls themselves,
beneath the dark rafters and the huge cross struts were
dozens of sketches and water-colours, showing Lorna's
wide range of skill, touched here and there by brilliance.

Leading off the studio was an alcove, where Lorna kept
stores of paint, canvas, thinners: everything needed for
her work. Beyond this, facing south over the river, was a
small room with a divan bed, a small dressing-table, and
a dozen smocks like those beloved by Josephine, two or
three pairs of slacks, slippers and sandals.

Lorna looked from the painting to the photographs,
then back to the painting, telling herself that she must be
mistaken, when she heard a ring at the front door bell.
The next moment she heard Josephine walk briskly out
of the kitchen to the door. Lorna was too preoccupied to

pay much attention—the caller was almost certainly a tradesman.

She heard a man say: 'Good morning. Mrs. John Mannering?'

That came of allowing Josephine to wear the studio smocks, she thought wryly.

'Yes,' Josephine said. She would add: 'Who shall I say wishes to see her?' and would then make an effort to recollect whether the loft-ladder was up or down; if up, then 'Mrs. Mannering' was out.

But those words did not come. Instead, Lorna heard a peculiar gasp, followed by silence. Lorna leaned forward, listening intently. There was a heavy thump and the loud slamming of the front door.

CHAPTER 3

VICTIM

LORNA leaned over the hatch opening and called: 'Josephine!' She heard nothing, and the quiet was unnerving. 'Josephine!' she called again; but only silence answered her. Thoroughly disquieted she darted towards the tiny alcove, where a small window overlooked the street and saw a man getting into a car about a hundred yards away. Almost instantaneously the car started off, too fast. A child on a cycle turned his wheel in alarm, bumped into the kerb and toppled over. The car disappeared.

Lorna flew towards the step-ladder again.

To get down it was safest to go backwards. Descending, she reproached herself for having delayed so long. Hurrying, she missed a step and hit the floor heavily, jolting her whole body. Momentarily, she was dizzy. Picking herself up she made her way with a greater deliberation towards the hall and the front door. Her slowness now was partly because she was afraid of what she might see.

Josephine lay almost flat on her back, her feet towards the door, her head towards Lorna. At first sight there was nothing the matter with her, but as she drew closer Lorna saw the crimson patch on her pale blue smock, just below the left breast.

'Oh no!' Lorna breathed.

She went still closer.

Josephine's right arm lay beneath her, awkwardly, her left fell naturally, the hand drooping; an attractive hand. There was no sign of movement at breast or lips, unless—

unless that crimson patch was spreading. Lorna went to the woman's side. In a way Josephine, with her dark hair and fresh, clear complexion, was attractive. Her face was in repose, the eyes nearly closed, the lips just parted. Lorna felt for her pulse, watching the crimson patch as if mesmerised. There was no movement at the wrist. With a futile gesture Lorna touched Josephine's forehead. Then she straightened up and went towards the telephone. Her fingers were not quite steady as she picked up the receiver and dialled Quinns' number.

A man's voice said: 'This is Quinns.'

'Is——' Lorna began, and broke off.

'This is Quinns, madam. Can I help you?'

'Is—Mr. Mannering in?'

'I'll see, madam, if——'

'This is Mrs. Mannering.'

'Mrs. Mannering, I do beg your pardon!' There was only a brief pause before John came on the line, the tone of his deep voice too care-free, too happy, against the background of what she had to say to him.

'Hallo, darling! Did I forget something?'

'John,' she said, and broke off. How *could* she say 'Josephine has been murdered in cold blood?'

'Lorna, what is it?' Mannering asked in a sharper tone. 'Are you all right?'

'Yes—no,' Lorna answered in a high, unnatural voice. 'Someone came to the door and stabbed—stabbed Josephine.' Over an exclamation which Mannering could not repress, she added: 'She's dead. I'm sure she's dead.'

Mannering was still and silent for what seemed a long time. Why didn't he say something? Why did he just not respond? Didn't he believe her?

At last he said: 'I'll be over at once, darling. Have you told the police?'

'No. I——'

'Are *you* all right?'

'Yes. Yes, I'm—I was up in the studio.'

'Keep the door locked and don't open it unless you're sure it's the police or me. Is that clear?'

'Yes. Yes. You'll hurry, won't you?'

'I won't lose a second,' Mannering promised. 'Make yourself some coffee—strong coffee, and put a lot of sugar into it.' He rang off immediately and Lorna put down the receiver and turned, her gaze falling involuntarily on Josephine lying so still. She moistened her lips, and tears stung her eyes; she moved almost blindly to the kitchen.

In his office, Mannering sat still except for a movement of his left hand, to press a bell-push three times. This was a signal for everyone in the shop to listen to him on the relay system which was used only in emergency. He saw the door open and Josh Larraby appear, obviously alarmed, as he spoke into the microphone.

'Josh, speak to Bristow at the Yard and tell him that the servant at my flat has been brutally attacked—it looks like murder. Ask him to have someone go there at once; Mrs Mannering is alone.' Josh Larraby's expression reflected his own shock but almost immediately he vanished. 'Lionel, go and get my car—you'll be coming with me. The others see that Mr. Rennie is told I won't be in again this morning, and cancel all today's appointments.'

Someone called: 'Very good, sir.'

Mannering pressed the bell-push again, cutting off the loud-speaker, smoothed his hair back, and sat still for at least two minutes. When he went outside, Larraby was coming off the other telephone.

'Mr. Bristow will go to Green Street himself, sir, and

Chelsea Division is being informed. I—I'm dreadfully sorry, sir.'

'Yes, Josh.' Mannering paused and Larraby waited. 'Do you know anything about Sir Cornelius Vandemeyer?'

'Nothing that isn't general knowledge, sir.'

'Did you hear any rumours on his marriage?'

'To Miss Deirdre Lanchester? None of significance, sir. There was a lot of talk about the disparity of their ages, the usual lewd suggestions that he would not live long! You know the kind of thing.'

'Yes, I know,' agreed Mannering. 'I want you to keep your ears very close to the ground about him, Josh. Whether he's been behaving out of character since his marriage. Whether he's been buying more heavily than usual; in other words, find out all you can about him.'

'Is it to do with this sad affair?' asked Larraby.

'I just want to know all there is to know about Vandemeyer,' Mannering said. 'Let it be assumed I'm interested in the way of business.'

'I'll do that,' promised Larraby.

At that moment the long, silver nose of the Jaguar slid into sight, and Mannering strode across the royal blue carpet which yielded under every step, reaching the door from this side as young Lionel reached it from the street. Several passers-by saw Mannering, and one woman whispered to her companion.

Lionel opened the door.

'Chelsea—and I'm really in a hurry,' Mannering said.

'*I'm* to drive, sir?' Lionel, delighted, shut Mannering in and darted to the other side of the car. Soon he was weaving his way through traffic with the expertise of youth, aware that there was trouble yet showing no sign of curiosity. He chose to go by a slightly longer route. Mannering noticed this, but his thoughts were on Lorna and how she must be feeling; and about Josephine.

The whole thing was absolutely unbelievable. It was almost as if he were being the victim of a hoax. That was absurd, of course, Lorna's voice had been quite unmistakable. But Josephine—*murdered*.

He was almost at the end of Green Street when he realised that he was virtually taking it for granted that Josephine had been killed in mistake for Lorna; also that subconsciously he had associated this with the mystery of Deirdre Vandemeyer. There was no process of reasoning, just an instinctive association of events and ideas.

They turned the corner.

Two police cars were already outside the house, and twenty or thirty people had gathered near, being kept away from the front door by two policemen who towered above them. The house itself stood tall above a row of newer, lower dwellings and a small block of flats. Mannering had lived here during the war when the buildings on either side had been bombed out of existence, and at one time this house had stood up from the street like a single tooth in a denuded lower jaw. Lionel Spencer tooted faintly, and a policeman indicated a clear place for him to pull into behind one of the cars.

'It's Mr. Mannering,' he said as he got out.

'Good morning, Mr. Mannering.'

''Morning. How long have you been here?' asked Mannering.

'Ten minutes or so, sir.'

'Everything all right?'

'Your wife's all right, I can tell you that, sir.'

'Thanks,' grunted Mannering. 'Doctor here yet?'

'No, sir, but he shouldn't be long now. Come with the ambulance, probably.'

Mannering nodded.

'Come up with me, Lionel,' he said. 'Just to stand by.'

'I will indeed, sir.'

There was a small lift, in which there was only room for two persons, and it climbed very slowly. As Lionel opened the door on the fifth and top floor, another policeman appeared. Beyond him the front door of the flat was open and men were moving about inside. One, with a camera, was standing almost on top of the body. Two others, with steel coil measures, were checking the distance between the extremities of the body and the door and walls of the room.

Because of the photographer, Josephine's face was uncovered, and death looked at Mannering starkly. He strode past the men, having to step over the body, and saw Lorna in the kitchen talking to a woman whom he only vaguely recognised as the tenant of a flat below. Lorna looked pale but unhurt. Her face lit up at the sight of Mannering, and the neighbour, elderly, grey-haired and plump, said hastily:

'Well, I won't stay, Mrs. Mannering. Do let me know if there is anything I can do.'

'You're very kind,' Lorna replied.

'Hallo, Mrs. Wilberforce,' Mannering said, summoning her name out of the recesses of his memory. 'How nice of you to come so quickly.'

'When I realised what had happened——' Mrs. Wilberforce began, and then she turned and hurried out, her voice failing her.

Mannering found himself in front of Lorna, gripping both her hands, looking closely into her eyes. He could see both the strain and the pain in them.

'Did you have that coffee?' he asked.

'I—no.'

'Let's put a kettle on,' Mannering said. He moved to

the sink, while Lorna turned to a cupboard. For a few moments they busied themselves with trifling things, as the men worked outside with a kind of controlled speed which achieved striking results in very little time.

At last, the coffee made, Lorna said: 'I was in the studio. There was a ring at the front door. Josephine...' She related everything that had happened almost like a recitation, as if she were still suffering from shock. Mannering sat on a corner of the kitchen table, while Lorna moved about with the coffee in her hand. When she finished she stopped in front of Mannering.

'John,' she said, '*Why?* Why Josephine?'

Mannering looked at her very straightly.

'This caller said: "Mrs. Mannering", didn't he?'

'Yes.'

'And Josephine said "Yes".'

'She didn't mean she was me, she meant——' Lorna broke off, and a puzzled expression clouded her eyes. 'It *sounded* as if she were saying she was me! Is that what you mean?'

'Doesn't it seem so to you?' asked Mannering.

He thought how very beautiful Lorna was, although in these moments of strain and anxiety her face was set in that sullen expression which deceived so many people. Her hair was brushed back more severely than usual, and threw her features into greater prominence. She sipped coffee, looking at him over the rim of her cup, and then said slowly:

'So you think she was killed in mistake for me.'

'I think we ought to assume she was until we can prove she wasn't,' said Mannering.

'Poor, poor Josephine,' said Lorna huskily. 'Poor woman. If she hadn't come here to work for me she would be alive.'

'Lorna,' Mannering said, almost sternly.

'Yes?'

'You're going to have to start thinking of yourself first.'

'As I am always telling you to do,' said Lorna, with a wry smile. 'How we are reversing the normal. You mean——' She broke off, but he did not help her, he was making sure that she reached her conclusions out of the recesses of her own mind. If she did, if she *believe*d that Josephine had been killed in mistake for her and was not simply told so by him, she would understand the significance more, would probably accept guidance and advice more readily.

'If she was—and I don't admit it yet, but if she was— then I'm still in danger.'

'Yes,' Mannering answered simply.

'And must be careful.'

'Extremely careful.'

'John,' Lorna said, 'it's hard enough to believe that Josephine *is* dead. It's much more difficult to believe that I'm in danger. Why should I be?'

A detective had moved from the hall towards the kitchen and obviously heard the last words. He stared in, and Mannering could sense the effort he made to restrain himself from following up Lorna's remark.

'I'll need to question Mrs. Mannering soon,' he said.

'Whenever you wish,' Mannering said. 'Come in.'

'Thank you, sir.'

'Have you heard anything about the car?' asked Lorna.

'No, Mrs. Mannering,' the man said. 'I sent out your description at once, of course, but these things take time. We've talked to the boy-cyclist, but he is only six, and isn't at all likely to help us. He didn't see the man or the car until it brushed him off his bike.' The detective turned to Mannering and went on: 'I'm Detective-Inspector Toller, sir—of the Chelsea Division. I understand that Mr. Bristow is on his way from the Yard and I delayed asking questions to save Mrs. Mannering from having to go over it again.'

As he spoke, there was another movement in the hall, and two men stepped from the lift. One of them was a stranger to Mannering, dark-faced, dark-eyed, alert-looking. The other was of medium height, with iron grey hair and very clear, pale grey eyes. He was immaculately dressed in a grey overcheck suit, and in his left lapel he wore a red gardenia.

This was Chief Superintendent Bristow, once Mannering's chief adversary, for long his close friend—and Lorna's, too.

CHAPTER 4

DEFERENCE

As Bristow entered the hall, every man stopped doing his job, and stood still with an unusual deference. Bristow, surprised, glanced about him and then appeared to realise that this was due to the announcement of his retirement. He raised his hand in a kind of mute acknowledgment, stepped over the body and came towards Mannering and Lorna. His eyes were bright, and despite the lines etched deeply round them, he looked youthful and very fit.

'Lorna,' he said, and held out his hand. He turned to Mannering. 'John, it was very thoughtful of you to telephone me this morning.' He paused, must have noticed Lorna's surprised glance, then went on: 'I couldn't be more sorry about this unhappy business.' He half-turned towards Toller, and drew him in with the smoothness of a diplomatic 'Have you made any progress, Inspector?'

Toller, short, broad, massive and brown-faced, pursed thick lips.

'Mrs. Mannering gave us a description of a man in a pale grey/brown suit getting into a white car and going off in a hurry,' he answered. 'We've been looking for the car, of course—there's a general call out.'

'Car number?' asked Bristow.

'I didn't get it,' Lorna said. 'I was trying to see the man and to make sure of the colour of his suit. I'm sorry.'

'White cars are two a penny, grey/brown suits——'

'It had a touch of green in it,' Lorna interpolated.

'With a touch of green are much more rare,' Bristow adjusted what he was going to say quickly. 'Anything else?' he asked Toller.

'Death appears to have been instantaneous, sir. Apparently there was one upward thrust with a knife-blade about an inch wide. I looked at the wound but haven't touched it. I had it photographed and then covered up.'

'Dr. Gogarty is here now, you can check with him,' said Bristow. 'Any fingerprints?'

'No, sir.'

'The man I saw was wearing gloves,' Lorna interrupted.

'John, the sooner you can help Lorna remember everything she saw the sooner we'll get our man,' Bristow said. 'Is there anything more you want Mrs. Mannering for now, Inspector?'

Toller hesitated. 'I would like a full statement as soon as possible, sir,' he said, formally. 'Mrs. Mannering has been good enough to state the most crucial facts, but hasn't yet made a statement.'

'I'm quite prepared to make a statement at any time,' Lorna interpolated. 'There isn't much more to tell.'

'Will you be present while the statement is made and recorded?' asked Bristow crisply. 'Let us know when you've finished.' He led Mannering out of the kitchen, like an officer going on parade. 'It's past time I retired,' he muttered into Mannering's ear. 'I'm a bad-tempered cuss these days.' A man passed them into the kitchen, carrying a small tape-recorder, and the door closed on him.

Bending over the body was the dark energetic-looking man—the police-surgeon, Gogarty. He was raising the shirt blouse carefully, and revealing the full, firm, marble-white belly, then the primly fitting brassiere. Beneath the left breast was the wound, surprisingly narrow and clean-looking, with a slight ridge and purply-blue discoloration surrounding it. A photographer stood near, bird-of-prey-like in his eagerness to take another picture.

Gogarty looked up. He had very sharp features, and was a striking-looking man, with a hooked nose and piercing brown eyes under beetling brows.

'Internal bleeding,' he announced. 'A single thrust by a man who knew his anatomy.'

'Or else struck lucky,' Bristow suggested.

'If he came to kill he wouldn't run away until he was sure he had,' reasoned Gogarty. 'I wouldn't call that luck.' He made that comment as he straightened up. 'I don't think I've ever seen a cleaner job.'

'See what you mean,' grunted Bristow.

'It might be a case of practice makes perfect,' Mannering remarked.

'Any reason to suggest that he has done it before?' Bristow demanded.

'Only a guess, based on Dr. Gogarty's confidence that he knew his anatomy.'

Bristow looked almost annoyed, and then gave a reluctant grin.

'The pair of you ought to solve this between you,' he said. 'I'm not needed. Do you know each other?'

'By name,' Mannering said.

'By reputation,' Gogarty replied.

They shook hands. Gogarty's was cold and his clasp quick and firm. There was a hint of nervous tension about him, as if he were fighting back a natural emotion of impulsiveness. His lips were particularly well-shaped although thin, and they had an upward curve at the corners, as if he often laughed; yet nothing else about him suggested this.

Ambulance men arrived, squeezing their way out of

the lift with a stretcher clutched between them. Mannering was glad of the chance to move away with Bristow
into the room which served as dining-room and study. He
perched on the settle where the press-cutting books stood,
recalling that Bristow had been mentioned in practically
every one of the earlier newspaper stories as the leader of
the Yard's fight against the Baron. Now he sat within feet
of his old adversary, lit a cigarette and looked at Mannering through the flame from his lighter. As he lowered it
and let the extinguishing cap fall, he asked quietly:

'Well, John. What do you know about this?'

'I'm not sure you're going to believe me,' Mannering
said. 'I think Josephine may have been killed in mistake
for Lorna.' He explained briefly, and went on: 'Let me
tell you everything which could have a bearing on it,
Bill—but remember I am guessing. I've nothing to go on
at all.'

'You used to call it a hunch,' Bristow remarked.

'So I did.' He laughed. 'What a lot of bright-sounding
names we use for jumping to conclusions! Now hear me
out, and tell me what you think when I've finished.' He
related the story from the moment that he had seen
Lorna looking through the photographs, what she had
said that morning, all her suspicion that the Lady Vandemeyer of Harrods was not the real Lady Vandemeyer.
During the recital, Bristow lit a cigarette from the butt of
the first, but otherwise made no movement and showed
no sign of belief or disbelief. As Mannering drew near
the end, Lorna came out of the kitchen, there were
background noises of Toller's 'Thank you, Mrs. Mannering,' and Lorna's: 'I don't think I've forgotten anything.'
She paused in the doorway of the dining-room and Mannering beckoned her in. She drew near Bristow, stopping
him from rising with a gesture, and listened intently, half-

frowning, as Mannering finished:

'... I know of absolutely no other reason for an attack on Lorna—still less for one on Josephine Smith.' He looked up at his wife. 'And you don't, darling, do you?'

'I can't *really* believe there can be any connection between this and Lady Vandemeyer,' Lorna said. 'I can't even begin to imagine that as a motive.' She turned impulsively to Bristow. 'Can you, William?'

Bristow took out the stub of the second cigarette and pressed it against an ashtray.

'If I stretch my imagination to its limit, just about,' he said gravely. 'Let me make sure I'm seeing this in exactly the same way as you are, John. You think Lorna is right: that the woman known as Lady Vandemeyer is a different person from the Lady Vandemeyer of four weeks ago. You think that after they met at Harrods, *that* Lady Vandemeyer or some associate, knowing how observant artists are, feared that Lorna had realised there was an impersonation. From this your reason that the murder of Josephine Smith was an attempt to kill Lorna and so make sure she didn't talk to anyone about the impersonation?'

'That's it in a nutshell,' Mannering approved.

'There's one little thing,' said Lorna tentatively.

'What colour?' asked Bristow, brightly.

'The Lady Vandemeyer I saw when painting her *was* the real one. She had been Deirdre Lanchester. I knew her too well to have any doubts about that. So the Harrods one was either very much changed *or* was someone impersonating Deirdre.' Lorna spread her hands in a helpless gesture. 'It isn't possible, is it?'

'Clearly possible,' Bristow said briskly. He stood up and gripped Lorna's arm in a firm, fatherly kind of way. 'Obviously there could be a lot of other explanations, but if I were in John's position I would see it as he does. And if I were in your position I would be very careful indeed. Very careful,' he added with emphasis.

Lorna stood utterly still.

Mannering said huskily: 'Yes. She will.' After a long pause, he went on: 'Bill, do you know anything at all to suggest that Cornelius Vandemeyer is in any kind of trouble?'

Bristow looked at him thoughtfully. 'None whatsoever.'

'Will you check closely?'

'As it's a line of inquiry into this murder, I most certainly will,' Bristow promised. 'And I'll keep you informed. Now I'd better have a word with young Toller and convince him that I am not going to take the case out of his hands.' He moved towards the door, smiling drily. 'John—one thing.'

'Yes?'

'Not a word of this must reach the newspapers: of the Vandemeyer angle, I mean.'

'It won't through us,' Mannering assured him. 'The press will assume that I'm involved in some case which has led to this, of course. Bill—one thing for you, too.'

'What is it?' Bristow raised his head and studied Mannering without appearing to do so.

'I am not involved in any other case. I know nothing more than I've told you. The most important matter on my mind until this happened was the question of selling part of Quinns so that I would be less tied to the business, and Lorna and I could travel together more.'

'I'm very glad to know it,' Bristow said, smiling faintly. 'All clear and understood, John. I haven't anything up my sleeve and you haven't anything on your conscience. But we've two problems and neither of us will be surprised if they turn out to be one and the same. You know this is likely to be my last major case, don't you?'

'I know,' Mannering said.

They shook hands, a quick, almost reflex, action on both their parts, and then Bristow turned and walked smartly out of the room. Lorna stood very still, looking at Mannering who moved towards her and put his arm round her shoulders. She drew a deep breath, and seemed to hold it for a long time. Then she freed herself, and spoke in a brisker, matter-of-fact tone.

'We have to get a message to Josephine's son.' Mannering hadn't given that a thought. 'He lives in Tottenham and works at Elstree Studios. I suppose it's a good thing she didn't see much of him, there was a mother-in-law feud.' Tears glistened in Lorna's eyes, and her voice nearly broke. 'John what a terrible thing if she *was* killed in mistake for me. What a thing to have on my conscience!'

'If you try to carry that on your conscience, you need a psychiatrist,' Mannering said, more sharply than he intended. 'The very idea's nonsense.'

After a pause, Lorna said: '*I* don't think it's nonsense.'

Suddenly, Mannering wished he had not spoken with such vehemence.

'I can see what you mean,' he said more mildly. 'But there isn't any true reason to blame yourself for a chance encounter in Harrods, is there? If you'd gone to the house and badgered her you might feel some responsibility. But a chance meeting—no, you can't blame yourself in the slightest.'

He thought Lorna's expression cleared a little.

'It sounds reasonable,' she conceded, 'but most arguments in one's own favour usually do. John, you will make every effort to find out who killed Josephine, won't you?'

'I will do absolutely everything I can,' Mannering promised. 'I've already started in fact. Josh is making inquiries about Cornelius Vandemeyer.'

This time there was no doubt that Lorna's expression cleared. There was no need to tell her that whatever he did would be far more to make sure she was not in danger, than to avenge Josephine.

The police would be here for some time yet, and she would certainly be safe for the next few hours.

'Why don't you get busy tracking down Josephine's son,' he suggested. 'Or would you rather the police did that?'

'I'd like to,' she answered at once. 'Have—have they taken her away yet?'

'I imagine so,' said Mannering. 'I'll go and make sure.'

When he stepped into the hall the body had gone, but men were still taking measurements and photographs. He had been at the scene of routine investigations like these a hundred times, but never ceased to be fascinated by the almost finicky attention to detail. One trifling clue over-looked might, in court, bring a police case down into little pieces. It was all necessary, yet seemed so cold-blooded.

Bristow came from the lift again, brisk as ever.

'I'd like Lorna to show me those photographs, John.'

'I'm sure she'll be glad to.'

'And don't worry about her,' Bristow said in an under-tone. 'I'll keep the place under surveillance and make sure she is watched wherever she goes.'

'Fine,' said Mannering. 'Fine.'

But his blood ran cold. Bristow would not take such precautions unless he felt—or in this case sensed—that the danger to Lorna was very real.

He went into the dining-room.

'Josephine's gone,' he said, quietly. 'Bill wants to go up to the studio with you. You won't go out without letting me know, will you?'

'No,' Lorna promised. She smiled; but it was the kind of smile which hid fear.

Whether there was any justification for them or not, these fears were felt keenly by three people not inclined to be fanciful or to imagine danger.

Mannering was in a very troubled and uneasy frame of mind when he went out, to find young Lionel Spencer watching a fingerprint expert with close attention on a landing two floors down. Lionel came hurrying at Mannering's call, looking a little shamefaced.

'Hope you haven't been calling me for long, sir.'

'Not too long. But when I say I want you standing-by, I mean it.'

'I'm sorry, sir. It—oh, it's no excuse.'

'What's no excuse?'

The boy looked into his eyes with glowing enthusiasm.

'You're used to it, sir, being a famous police consultant, but this is wholly new to me. A police investigation into a murder. It's a wonderful chance—one in a million, sir.'

'Yes,' Mannering said drily. 'No doubt it is.'

One chance in a million—and the fact that a woman had been killed was the cause of Lionel Spencer's wonderful opportunity! Happily oblivious to this macabre side of it, Lionel appeared to be quite content to ride passenger as Mannering drove; for now Mannering wanted to have to concentrate on driving—somehow manoeuvring through traffic always sharpened his wits.

It was nearly one o'clock when he pulled up outside Quinns. He got out and sent Lionel to park the car, paused outside the window to admire a jade casket so intricately carved that he could only marvel at the years of patient work by the Chinese craftsman who had wrought it out of a single piece of stone.

Then he saw Larraby approaching from inside the shop and could tell from the expression on the old man's face that he had news about Cornelius Vandemeyer.

Lionel Spencer was in his seventh heaven, its brightness dimmed only momentarily when Mannering had rebuked him for not standing by. He had known of Mannering and Quinns for years, and without Mannering having the faintest idea, had hero-worshipped him as a kind of Scarlet Pimpernel and Beau Brummel combined. He had studied antiques and allied trades in his spare time, and so qualified himself, when the opportunity came, for the job at Quinns. If he overdid anything it was his attempt to imitate the Regency dandy. He dressed in the latest, most trendy, fashion, elegant and almost foppish; and he also trained himself to the peak of physical fitness, as well as qualifying in both judo and karate.

He was pleasant-looking, pleasant-mannered, and had one very great advantage over most people, an inherited fortune. So he could do what work he liked, and he was doing what he had dreamed of most of his life: working with the fabulous John Mannering.

Now he felt he had taken a great stride forward: he was on a case with Mannering. He did not know much about it yet, but sensed its importance, and if he needed any confirmation it was the way both Larraby and Mannering looked as they met in the doorway of Quinns.

CHAPTER 5

WORD FROM THE GRAPE-VINE

JOSHUA LARRABY was a man with a remarkable history. Apprenticed to a gold- and jewel-smith, he had spent half of his life in the obscurity of a safe job with sufficient to live on, but a passion had been born in him—a passion which had become a mania.

He had learned to love precious stones as most men love a woman, with single-hearted devotion and compelling desire. Their beauty first fascinated, then hypnotised, finally seduced him, until he had stolen gems of surpassing beauty—not for financial gain but simply for love of them. Naturally, he had been caught, tried and sentenced to three years' imprisonment. When he came out of prison he had no settled way of life, or work, to go back to, yet the years of loneliness and privation had not enabled him to repress his love of jewels.

He had, inevitably, been on the fringe of the underworld, and on that fringe had one day met a man who had transformed his whole life. John Mannering of Quinns. Mannering had given him a job among the very things he so loved: jewels, *objets d'art*, antiques. Over the years, his loyalty and trustworthiness had brought full reward: he managed Quinns of London and he had won the respect and trust both of the trade and of the police—*and* of the half-world of thieves and fences and their families. Everybody liked old Josh. Everybody knew he could be trusted. And everybody was glad to give him little choice bits of information; the grape-vine of the world of art and jewel thieves and fences was always full of information for Josh Larraby.

Whatever he had learned today would be absolutely reliable; Mannering was quite sure of that.

He turned into his office, and Larraby followed, closing the door. It was a small room, with a beautifully bowed Queen Anne desk, white-painted shelves of reference books on antiques, jewellery and *objets d'art* behind the desk. Above his head, a portrait of a cavalier—who might have been his twin. In fact Lorna had painted it, of him, nearly twenty years before. In a far corner was a deep seated winged armchair; it stood over a covered entrance to the strong room beneath the shop.

'Sit down, Josh,' Mannering said, and Larraby chose a wooden armchair in front of the desk. 'What have you discovered?'

'Cornelius Vandemeyer has of late been buying pictures and *objets d'art* knowing them to be stolen,' Larraby stated flatly.

Mannering stared, as Larraby shifted his chair to one side.

'Heavily?' asked Mannering at last.

'I imagine so—that is the impression I was given,' Larraby answered.

'How long has it been going on?'

'Two or three weeks,' said Larraby.

'*Weeks,*' echoed Mannering. 'No more?'

'If the details of my information are correct, he is said to have wanted the set of Dutch miniatures stolen in the Addering House burglary,' said Larraby, 'and paid a good price for them. If you'll forgive me pointing it out, sir, Sir Cornelius has a remarkable collection of miniatures.

'Quite remarkable,' Mannering murmured, not mak-

ing it clear to which factor he referred. 'Yes. It sounds
reasonable, except——' He pursed his lips.

'Sir Cornelius's wealth, sir?' objected Larraby.

'Yes, that's what I boggle at.'

'But money could not have bought the Addering Collection, sir.'

'No,' agreed Mannering, still absently. 'No. How well
do you know Vandemeyer?'

'I don't really *know* him at all,' Larraby replied.

'If to know means a certain degree of intimacy,' said
Mannering, 'nor do I. His reputation however is public
property. Scrupulously honest, exceedingly rich, chairman
of several charity committees which have a world-wide
reputation. We know these things. American nationality
with Dutch forebears, one of the world's most respected
bankers, with substantial holdings in oil and natural gas
companies. Three times married. His first wife divorced
him, his second one died in a plane crash. He married
Deirdre Lanchester about eighteen months ago. I think
somewhere along the line there is a daughter.'

Mannering paused.

'I knew less than that about his domestic affairs,' said
Larraby.

'I don't know enough, and know very little about him
as a person,' Mannering replied. 'What do you make of it,
Josh?'

'If I may say so, sir, I don't know what has aroused your
interest.' Larraby looked almost apologetic.

'You don't——' began Mannering, and then laughed
ruefully. 'Of course you don't—I'd forgotten.' His amuse-
ment faded and his expression became grave and set as he
explained. The story took a long time in telling and
Mannering saw the changing emotions on the fine old
face, sensed how Josh's mind began to work. When he

had finished, Larraby leaned forward, hands clasped on the desk.

'The coincidence of timing is quite remarkable, sir.'

'Yes. Until a few weeks ago, his wife led a normal, social life, and there was not a whisper against Vandemeyer. Suddenly, she withdraws because of a so-called illness, and about the same time he appears on the under-world market. It's almost too much for coincidence, Josh.'

'It is indeed, sir. May I say how very sorry I am that Mrs. Mannering appears to be a victim of such circumstances. At least you are now warned and can take precautions. If you feel you should spend more time with her, sir, I can cope very well here.'

'I'm sure you can,' Mannering said. 'But I don't think she would want me under her feet all day. And she is anxious to find out who killed Josephine Smith.' Mannering went on. 'I don't yet know what I'm going to do, Josh—but I know I want to learn more about Vandemeyer. When the story of the murder breaks I'll be in the headlines so I can't take a personal interest in Vandemeyer. Now! I want you to go to the major dealers today and tomorrow, looking for miniatures and pictures in enamel and medallions—the three things Vandemeyer collects most avidly. You can hint that you have an overseas buyer, Vandemeyer is bound to crop up in conversation, and you should learn if he's been in the market at all, or is showing any special interest in any particular kind of *objet*. You will even find out if he's stopped buying through the normal channels.'

Larraby's eyes were glowing.

'I'm bound to learn a great deal, sir. Would you like me to start at once?'

'Yes.'

'I will report to Chelsea this evening,' Larraby promised, and went out.

Mannering sent Lionel Spencer for some sandwiches, and the youth brought them in with coffee brewed in a little kitchen at the back of the shop. Lionel took such obvious pleasure in the trifling service that Mannering watched him thoughtfully as he went out—and then promptly put him out of his mind. He had to concentrate on routine work and on getting his desk clean in case he had to spend a lot of time away from it. There was a note that Brian Rennie was due at half-past two. With luck, each would be able to keep the appointment this time.

Routine and lunch finished, he found himself pondering over Lorna's story. It wasn't surprising that she had remembered colours more vividly than anything else, and in the long run a description of the murderer's clothes might be more useful than details of the car. Grey/brown with a touch of green.

At half-past two precisely, Rennie arrived.

Rivalling Lionel Spencer, he was exquisitely dressed in a green corduroy suit with pale brown tie, gloves, shoes and socks. In his middle forties, he looked what the old world would have called a fop and the new world would have suspected of being a 'queer'. Nothing could have been more wrong. He had a wife of whom he was exceedingly fond, and three lusty children. The movement as he put out his hand was almost effeminate—but his grip was like iron.

'I'm sorry I was late this morning, John.'

'It suited me very well,' said Mannering.

'I might have guessed you would say that,' said Rennie. They went into the office and Mannering waved to the big armchair. Rennie sat down, hitching up his trousers with the care and precision with which a woman avoids 'seating' her skirt. Mannering took the chair behind the desk. 'All I want,' Rennie went on easily, 'is fifty-one per cent in Quinns of Boston, and forty-nine per cent of Quinns in Paris and here in London!'

'And how much would you be prepared to pay for it?' asked Mannering drily.

Rennie smiled. He had a long, delicately curved face, but his eyes were surprisingly hard.

'One million pounds,' he answered. 'The share for Paris in French credits, the share for Boston in dollars, and the share for this shop in any currency you wish.'

Mannering stared at him, thrust suddenly into turmoil. The price offered was at least twice what he would have asked had he been seriously thinking of selling, nearly three times as much as he would have settled for. Rennie watched him, smiling faintly, but his eyes held no smile.

'Is it a deal?' he asked.

Mannering hesitated, and then said: 'Not yet.'

'I can't wait for long,' said Rennie. 'I shall be flying back to New York tomorrow, and I want to take your answer with me.'

Mannering pursed his lips. His mind was still reeling under the impact of those figures. A *million* pounds—and he could do what he liked for the rest of his life: work here at Quinns or have someone stand in for him, spend more time with Lorna——

He shook his head, in sudden decision.

'Then the answer has to be "no",' he said.

'Because I want your decision quickly?'

'Yes.'

Rennie laughed. 'I should have known I couldn't rush you into anything even with a dazzling offer.'

'Why so dazzling?' asked Mannering. He smiled more

broadly. 'If anyone else had made it I would have assumed that some of my stock has unsuspected value.'

'It has,' said Rennie.

'I usually know,' Mannering replied.

'You couldn't know two things that I do,' said Rennie. 'There are two foundations in the States, one in California and one in Texas, which want to establish a unique English collection and will pay substantially for it. They might not buy everything I recommend so I would be taking a chance, but'—he hesitated—'sure you won't change your mind?'

'Not at a moment's notice,' Mannering said, almost sadly.

'Yet you might consider doing a deal,' Rennie said, thoughtfully.

'Yes I'm no uninterested,' Mannering admitted.

'How long would you want to make up your mind?'

Mannering did not answer—partly because he did not want to think seriously about anything but Vandemeyer and the possible danger to Lorna. That might be over in a day or two but it could go on for weeks, even longer.

'A month?' urged Rennie.

Mannering put his hands flat on the desk, and laughed.

'I'm sorry, Brian, but you've come at a time when I don't really want to think seriously about this or anything else, except——' He broke off, temped to tell Rennie why, yet seeing no reason why he should burden the other man with the story.

'It is a *very* substantial offer,' Rennie interrupted. 'Are you involved in one of your periodic adventures, John?'

'You might say so, yes.'

'Then wouldn't you be wise to come to terms quickly?' suggested Rennie. 'You would leave Lorna very well cared for, if anything went wrong. And by the law of average, something is bound to sooner or later. I don't wish to be a Jeremiah,' Rennie added hastily, 'but as an insurance, this offer is surely attractive.' He paused, hopefully.

Mannering said: 'I think I'll have to tell you what I'm worried about at the moment.'

He told Rennie without going into too great a detail, saw how Rennie reacted, obviously shaken and concerned. As he finished, he pointed out: 'So any decision I might make now would be under too much stress. I'm tempted to say "yes" so that I can concentrate on this problem, but that would be a panic-measure.'

'There isn't too much panic in accepting a million pounds while retaining control of two thirds of the business,' Rennie said drily. 'But I do understand, John. I would hate to be caught up in a situation like this. Don't you think Lorna should take a holiday? She would be very welcome to come to us in New York.'

'I wish she would go but can't imagine she will,' said Mannering. 'Nice of you, though.'

'John,' said Rennie. 'Are you seriously interested in my offer? Really?'

'Yes,' said Mannering flatly. 'Enough to consider it seriously.'

'Can't you give me a time limit?' Rennie leaned back in his chair again looking at Mannering through lowered lids. 'Surely a month would be long enough for you to make up your mind one way or the other.'

It certainly would be, Mannering thought. The uncertainty about Lorna shouldn't be allowed to drag on for anything like four weeks. If it did, then he, Mannering, would need to concentrate all his time and energy on that. And he wasn't being asked to sell everything, remember, and would retain control of Quinns here and in Paris. It was unlikely that he would ever have such a good offer again.

'Yes,' he said at last. 'I'll decide within a month. Will that suit you?'

'If I cable my Texan and Californian friends that I need a month for certain negotiations they'll allow the extension,' Rennie said confidently. 'Thank you, John. I wish you had made a snap decision but I quite understand why you didn't.' He sat up in his chair again, pursing his lips. 'Can I do anything at all to help you with the problem of Lorna?'

'You're very kind,' Mannering said, 'but I don't think so.'

'Who is involved?' asked Rennie. 'I may know something that will help. You would be surprised how much Londoners confide in me—in Americans generally for that matter. We're birds of passage and never likely to appear at moments which could be embarrassing.'

'It must be confidential,' Mannering said.

'Or *I* might say something indiscreet?'

'Yes,' said Mannering. 'Even you!'

Rennie laughed with obvious enjoyment, stood up, studied the portrait of the cavalier, which he had seen often before, and shook his head slowly.

'Lorna is remarkably talented. I know of no better living portraitist. I should hate——' He broke off, looked straight into Mannering's eyes, and then went on in a different tone: 'John, let me stand in for you here while you concentrate on your personal problems. I would learn a great deal about the business, and—but that possibility would probably be enough to make you say "no".' He broke off, wryly. 'Forget it, John.'

Very slowly, Mannering said: 'But I'm not at all sure I

want to forget it. Sit down, let's have some tea and think this over.'

Rennie laughed with unexpected gaiety.

'The Englishman's panacea,' he said. 'Very well, we shall have some tea and think this over!'

Mannering spoke to Lionel Spencer on the internal telephone, ordered tea, and made a quick mental check of the stock here, its value, the list of customers, the 'special customers' for whom Quinns was seeking particular items. It would not really matter if everyone in the business knew these things. What could matter was that in order to learn and to stand in for him, Rennie would have to know all the secrets of Quinns. There were safety precautions which no one dreamed of unless they were told. For instance, the fact that the chair covering the trap-door leading to the strong-room, on which Rennie was now sitting, could only be shifted more than an inch or two by pressing the right button at Mannering's side. There were a dozen such secrets, and only he and Larraby knew them all.

He could trust Rennie absolutely, of course.

Couldn't he?

There was a tap at the door and, as Mannering called 'come in' the telephone began to ring. He picked up the receiver, and said:

'Mannering of Quinns.'

'John,' said Bill Bristow, 'I've some news for you. Can you come and see me within the next hour?'

CHAPTER 6

NEWS FROM BRISTOW

'YES,' said Mannering. 'I'll be with you at'—he glanced at a French clock on a corner shelf; it was twenty to four —'a quarter past four.'

'Don't be later,' Bristow urged, and rang off.

By the time Mannering had put down the receiver, Lionel had brought the tea-tray and departed. Rennie was ostentatiously looking at an illustrated catalogue of a sale at an Elizabethan manor house in Cheshire, one of several catalogues on a table by the side of the winged chair. As Mannering started to pour out, he began to hitch the chair forward.

'That's too heavy,' Mannering said, taking tea to him. He proffered a plate of chocolate biscuits and some plain ones but Rennie waved them away. 'I have about twenty minutes,' he went on. 'Do you really have the time to spend a month here?'

'I certainly have,' Rennie assured him. 'I can hardly wait to find out all the secrets of Quinns! It has the reputation of being the best protected privately-owned shop in the world, although we in the States know a little about burglary precautions and crook-proof vaults!' He spoke so disarmingly that Mannering warmed to him.

'If I call you about seven o'clock this evening, will you be in?'

'I will. I've an evening of letter writing, and will be dining in my room.'

'Then I'll call you,' Mannering promised. 'You're very patient.'

'My dear John! You're half-ready to sell and three quarters ready to let me loose among the treasures here. I would be a lot more patient for half the chance!'

Five minutes later he left Quinns.

Five minutes after that Mannering set out for Scotland Yard, on foot.

Bristow's office was now in the new building, near Lambeth Bridge, ten minutes farther away than the old building near Westminster Bridge, but Mannering had half-an-hour to walk it in, which would be ample time. He strode through Hart Row, across Piccadilly, and then into Green Park and, very soon, St. James's. Normally he would have reflected on the green pleasance of the parks and even lingered by the lake, as much to watch the delight of children in the many-hued ducks and water-fowl, as to study them and relax. Today, however, he was too preoccupied to do more than enjoy the clean, crisp air. He reached Birdcage Walk, crossed to the western side of Parliament Square, and by back ways continued on to the new building of the Metropolitan Police. He did not really like this building. It would always, for him, lack the sense of stability and tradition of the old place in Scotland Yard, though younger men on the Force might scoff at such a sentiment.

There was a welcome sight in an elderly sergeant on duty in the bright, new hall.

'Good afternoon, Mr. Mannering. It's a long time since I've seen you.'

'I wish I had as good a memory as yours,' said Mannering.

'No reason for you to remember me, sir. Roberts—Sergeant Charlie Roberts. I used to drive Mr. Bristow sometimes. He says, will you go straight along, sir?'

'Thank you,' Mannering said.

He wasn't quite sure that he knew the way, but it was at least worth finding out how good his memory was. First floor, by lift or stairs—the lift was engaged—he chose the stairs. Ah! Turn right and two or three doors farther on—there it was! 'Chief Supt. W. E. Bristow'. Mannering tapped, and almost at once Bristow opened the door.

'Come in, John,' he said.

Mannering had often visited this man, outwardly calm but inwardly agitated and afraid of what Bristow might have discovered about his most recent activities. But he had never been more troubled and anxious than he was now. Bristow led the way to an angular desk and waved to an angular but surprisingly comfortable armchair, then rounded the desk and sat down.

'There's a limit to what I can tell you,' he said without preamble. 'But I've had a man checking closely, and I've reason to believe that Vandemeyer is in some kind of trouble.'

'Financial trouble?' asked Mannering quietly.

'If you mean has he lost his fortune—no, there's nothing to suggest that he isn't as wealthy as ever. But there's a lot to suggest that he is acting out of character. In fact, acting as a man might if he were being blackmailed.'

'Ah,' breathed Mannering. 'And I mustn't ask how you gathered that impression?'

Bristow said slowly. 'The entire household staff was given three months wages in lieu of notice, about the time Lady Vandemeyer fell ill.'

Mannering's breath came quickly. 'My God! Do you realise what you're saying?'

Bristow shrugged. 'Obviously it could have been to make sure that none of them noticed any change in Lady Vandemeyer, who was confined to her room with an unspecified illness for about ten days. The staff change took place during those ten days. Vandemeyer's valet and general factotum, a man who had served him most of his life, was the last one to be seen at the house by tradesmen.'

'Not Gillespie?' Mannering asked.

'I wondered if you knew him. Yes. He knew a lot about his employer's collecting, I gather.'

'He came to Quinns now and again,' Mannering said. 'And I've known him buy at the sale rooms for Vandemeyer. Where is he now?'

'No one appears to know,' Bristow answered.

'You mean——'

'I am not implying that he may not be alive,' interrupted Bristow drily. 'I simply know that he left, and no one knows where he went. He has no known family, no friends outside his employer and the staff.' Bristow shrugged.

'What about his personal belongings? Had he any home except with Vandemeyer?'

'No,' answered Bristow. 'He's worked for Vandemeyer for over thirty years, remember.'

'His home and his life have been built around Vandemeyer and his household,' Mannering observed heavily. 'He must hate Vandemeyer for throwing him out at a moment's notice.'

'That wouldn't be surprising,' Bristow agreed. 'We could find out a lot if we could talk to him.'

'Are you looking for him officially?'

Bristow took a cigarette from an open box of fifty on his desk, lit it, and answered:

'Yes, though I've no ostensible reason to suspect Vandemeyer of any crime, and I'm conducting the line of inquiry very discreetly. I thought you ought to know what I've discovered already.'

'Thanks,' said Mannering warmly. 'We know that something out of the ordinary happened at Vandemeyer's place about three or four weeks ago, but we haven't the slightest idea what it was. Do you know anything about the staff who've replaced those who were fired?'

'They all seem to be all right, but we're checking,' Bristow answered.

'Has Gillespie been replaced?'

With great deliberation, Bristow said: 'No, John. He will be a very difficult man to replace. I can tell you that Saxon's, the Agency which has supplied his staff in the past, are on the lookout for someone.'

Mannering went very still.

'If you see what I mean,' added Bristow, without a change of expression.

Slowly, Mannering replied: 'I see exactly what you mean. Vandemeyer needs a man he knows he can trust, who is knowledgeable about miniatures and *objets d'art* generally and who knows the trade. And we want someone who can get close enough to Vandemeyer to find out what is happening, someone uninhibited by official rules and regulations.'

'Right,' said Bristow, smiling almost frostily. 'There's another requirement, however.'

'What's that?'

'Vandemeyer mustn't be able to recognise the replacement.'

'No,' said Mannering. 'No.'

They sat silent for some minutes but there was no quiet in Mannering's mind. He now knew exactly why Bristow had asked him to call, and what Bristow hoped he would do. At first thought it seemed utterly impossible, but was it?

Bristow knew that there was no man in the world more capable of disguising himself than Mannering. He could be two different men virtually within an hour; in the past his expertness at disguise had, time and time again, saved him from capture and disaster. The moment he had realised the significance of Gillespie's disappearance Bristow must have thought: 'John Mannering could replace him.'

It meant other things, too.

Bristow was extremely anxious to find out what was happening in Vandemeyer's house, and this could only be because he suspected something both grave and unlawful. No doubt, too, he was influenced by the murder of Josephine.

'I'll think about it,' Mannering said, slowly.

'Don't take too long,' advised Bristow. 'Vandemeyer might fill the post, if you do.'

First Rennie, now Bristow, trying to pressure him into making a quick decision. Mannering was aware of the irony of that and saw its humour, but he wasn't in a mood to laugh. A dozen thoughts were flashing through his mind at once, and each of them came back to Lorna.

If he took on this task, how could he personally help to protect her?

He smiled drily at the thought that he was taking it for granted that if he wanted the vacant post with Vandemeyer he could have it. That was a long way from certain, and was a challenge in itself.

'The very idea is absurd,' declared Mannering.

'Ludicrous,' agreed Lorna, solemnly.

'Bristow can't have been serious,' Mannering declared.

'He was pulling your leg, darling.'

'No policeman in his right mind *could* be serious.'

'He was daring you to do something he knew you couldn't possibly attempt,' said Lorna. 'And if you did you would almost certainly fail.'

'Oh,' said Mannering. 'Was he?'

'And in any case you wouldn't dream of doing such a thing.'

'It's *years* since I put on a disguise, remember.'

'You've almost forgotten how,' Lorna said, straight-faced.

'Damn it, this *isn't* a joking matter!' protested Mannering.

'No, darling, I can see how serious you are.'

'Lorna——'

'And just a teeny-weeny bit devious,' Lorna declared; her eyes were laughing at him but her voice was serious.

'I am *not*, even the slightest bit, devious,' stated Mannering flatly.

'Aren't you, darling?' Didn't you know perfectly well the moment Bristow put this idea into your head that you would take Vandemeyer's job if you could possibly get it? And aren't you scheming like mad to make *me* talk you into it?'

Mannering looked at her for a moment in silence, and then laughed with sudden and complete good-humour.

'Believe it or not,' he said, 'but I hadn't realised it. I suppose you're right.'

He moved across the dining-room and put his arm around her. She looked up into his face, her expression more serious than before—as if his laughter had taken away the mood of teasing. He stood back from her, still holding her shoulders, and went on:

'I can't possibly do it, of course.'

'Why not?' she asked.

'I can't leave you, for a start. And——'

'No,' she said. 'I'm going to leave *you*.'

Again he looked at her, this time without understanding.

'John,' Lorna said. 'I've been thinking on and off all day about Josephine. I never seriously doubted that she was killed in mistake for me, and I suppose I've taken it for granted that they will try again. They *are* likely to, aren't they?'

'There's certainly a real danger,' Mannering agreed.

'So—it's silly to stay here and feel that I might be attacked at any moment,' Lorna went on. 'I suppose if the truth be told, I'm scared. I know nothing on this earth will stop you from trying to find out who killed Josephine and why, and if you were always looking over your shoulder in case I was in trouble, you couldn't really concentrate on the investigation, could you?'

'I would make quite sure you weren't in danger.'

'I know you'd try to,' Lorna corrected. 'It would be much better if I went off somewhere, and I've wanted to spend a few days in New York for some time. I think those portraits I did for the New Arts Society need varnishing and I'd loathe anybody else to touch them. I'd love to see the new exhibition at the Guggenheim and the Modern Art Museum, too. I could go off tomorrow. I've no very pressing commitments—the Cobe portrait being indefinitely deferred—and it won't take long to pack. As a matter of fact I would like to buy a few summer clothes in New York.' She paused for a moment and then went on rather quickly: 'I've made up my mind, John; please don't try to dissuade me.'

She was, he could see, making it possible for him to devote himself wholeheartedly to the Vandemeyer problem, and he knew as well as she that there was nothing he would like more.

CHAPTER 7

DISGUISE

MANNERING watched the VC10 climbing into the sky, dark trails from the jet engines like the exhaust of rockets. About him on the Observation Roof at London Airport were dozens of people—tearful relatives, solitary wives, here and there an airport official, and here and there an airport policeman and a plainclothes man from Scotland Yard.

The aircraft became a speck against the azure blue of the clear sky.

Mannering turned and went down to the main building of the Ocean Terminal and walked over partly-made roads and paths towards a multi-story car park. He took the wheel of Lorna's car, a Morris 1800, looking intently about him, but no one showed any interest. As he drove off he watched in the mirror but no one followed him. Once on the Great West Road he felt fairly secure, but from time to time he checked to make sure.

When he reached his flat he parked the car outside and a plainclothes man—one of a team on duty there since the murder—came up.

'Any problems?' asked Mannering.

'No, sir, nothing at all. Mrs. Mannering hasn't come out.'

Mannering kept a straight face.

'That's good,' he said.

There was an exit out of this building into the next and Lorna had left that way, obviously unnoticed—and if the police had not known, then no one else was likely to suspect. In a buoyant mood he went up in the tiny lift, let himself into the flat with a key, and stood for a moment on the threshold.

There was stillness and silence, as there should be. But the thought of its emptiness, and the reason, had a sudden, depressing effect. Depression wasn't easy to throw off but as he bustled about the flat, it lifted.

Up in the studio was a box of theatrical make-up, ostensibly there for Lorna and her sitters, actually for him. It was a long time since he had used it, except for a masked ball. He opened it and sat before a mirror in the alcove where Lorna kept her own paints and cleaning materials. He examined himself closely, deciding what best to do, then took off his coat and put one of Lorna's smocks round his shoulders.

As he made to sit down again, the telephone bell rang. There was an extension in the main studio, and he moved to it.

'John Mannering.'

'Just a moment, please, Mr. Bristow wants you.'

He waited, patiently.

It was two days since he had talked to Bristow about the Vandemeyer post, and a great deal had been planned and arranged in those two days. He wondered what specific thing Bristow was concerned about now.

'John ... Sorry to keep you.' Bristow was his brisk self. 'You'll be glad to know that no one followed you to or from the airport, and no one took any particular notice of you there. Our chaps didn't see Lorna leave Green Street, either.'

'That's fine,' Mannering said. 'Have you talked to the New York police?'

'Yes. They will watch Lorna on arrival at the Kennedy

Airport and see that she isn't followed from there,' Bristow assured him. 'You needn't worry at all.'

'Thank you, Bill,' Mannering said quietly.

'Glad to do it,' Bristow said. 'Now—Saxon's are expecting you this afternoon at three-thirty, I gather.'

'Yes,' Mannering said. 'I telephoned them yesterday, saying I was a John Marriott who has worked for a number of galleries in Europe and the United States.' As he spoke he changed the inflection of his voice, and sounded faintly American. 'How will that do, Bill?'

'I ought to have put you in prison twenty years ago,' Bristow said drily. 'I want to be kept in close touch. Don't forget.'

'I shan't forget it,' Mannering assured him.

When he rang off, he dialled Quinns, and almost immediately Larraby answered.

'Is Mr. Rennie there?' Mannering asked, in the faintly American voice.

'I'll find out, sir. Who is that, please?'

In the same accent, Mannering said: 'John Mannering —*alias* John Marriott.'

'John Mannering——' began Larraby, and then gave a little, delighted laugh. 'You quite fooled me, sir. I'll get Mr. Rennie at once.'

Mannering waited for only a few seconds, before Rennie came on the line.

'Hello, John! Did everything go off all right?'

'Perfectly,' Mannering said. 'Lorna will be well on the way to Johannesburg by now.' No one, barring Bristow, had been told where she was really going. 'How are things with you?'

'Fine—just fine. Larraby is a great help, but you know that.'

'You can trust him absolutely,' Mannering said. 'And if

you want to get a message through to me, do it through him.'

'My, my, how mysterious can you get!'

Mannering chuckled and rang off.

Slowly, he moved towards the alcove, as slowly sat down in front of the mirror. Then he began to cream his face in preparation for make-up, and with infinite pains he started the transformation. As he changed facially, so a subtle change seemed to take place in him: a metamorphosis which carried him back over twenty years to the time when he had sat in the make-up room of an artist in theatrical make-up and had watched the change wrought in himself.

First, the cleansing; next, a cream to rub in so that it darkened his skin to a deep tan, actually changing the colour. Next, gum at the corners of his eyes which narrowed them and caused tiny lines to appear at the corners, and aged him ten years in a matter of minutes. The gum set quickly, but it would be hours before he got used to it. Above all, he must not touch it with his fingers.

Next he put rubber suction pads into his cheeks; they held themselves into position and made his face look a little plumper. Then with infinite care, he inserted warmed wax into his nostrils to give them a slight distension.

He *was* a different man!

He used a plastic paint to make his teeth look slightly yellow, then began to work on his hair, using a cold water dye which made the streaks of grey much more noticeable. He ought to have had a haircut, but there wasn't time to seek out a man whom he could trust.

Finished, he peered at himself.

'Not bad,' he said aloud. 'Not bad at all.'

He added a few finishing touches before putting the make-up case away. There was a smaller one downstairs which he could take with his luggage. He went down, packed two dark suits and enough clothes for a week, and went out. Outside in the street, the detective who had talked to him when he had arrived, looked at him curiously but did not speak.

Mannering walked within two feet of him, and not the slightest hint of recognition showed.

Mannering took a bus which went along the Cromwell Road, and got off near the BEA terminal. He went into a small hotel, one of a dozen nearby, and a faded-looking clerk took him up to a first floor back room, overlooking narrow gardens which were mostly paved and tidy.

'This is the only room we have free with a private bath, sir.'

'This will suit me,' Mannering said. There was a double divan bed, a built-in wardrobe cupboard and a small dressing-table. 'How much is it?'

'On weekly terms, twenty guineas, sir. Or——'

'I'd like it for one week, anyway,' Mannering said.

'Thank you, sir. Will you sign the register next time you're down?'

'Yes,' Mannering promised.

He unpacked his few things, then scrutinised his make-up again. His skin needed a little darkening on one cheek, but otherwise there seemed nothing wrong. For the first time since seeing Lorna off, he really relaxed.

It was a quarter past two.

He went down, registered as John Marriott, and went out. On the other side of the road was a parade of small shops, one of them a café. He ordered minestrone soup, a plain omelette, cheese, biscuits and coffee. Only half-a-dozen customers were there, and no one took any notice of him. He was becoming used to his new guise, adjusting his mood and his manner to fit it. He paid the bill and went out, walking towards the Museums and Knightsbridge.

Saxon's Employment Bureau was in Knightsbridge, nearly opposite Harrods, where Lorna had encountered 'Lady Vandemeyer'. And Vandemeyer's house was also in Knightsbridge but behind Harrods, in Ellesmere Square.

At three twenty-four Mannering turned into the narrow doorway marked *Saxon's*. A door led to an estate agency on the left, and a flight of narrow steps led upwards to a brightly-lit landing. Mannering went up and found a door marked: *Inquiries*. He tapped and went in. A plump, bright-looking girl smiled up at him from a crowded office, two walls of which were lined with filing cabinets.

'Good afternoon.'

'My name is Marriott. I have an appointment——'

'Oh yes,' the girl interrupted. 'Mr. Saxon is expecting you. I won't keep you a moment.' She jumped up, showing a long expanse of well-developed leg, and disappeared into an inner room. Mannering heard her speaking as he looked about. Between him and the office was a counter with a flap in it; to get into the inner sanctum he would have to raise the flap and go through.

The girl reappeared, and raised the flap.

'Will you go in, please?' She looked at him with unfeigned interest.

Mannering went into a slightly larger office which was filled with card-index files and cabinets. Behind a small desk was a man with owlish-looking eyes and a baby face, small, pursed lips, and a wrinkled forehead. He half-rose from his chair.

'Sit down,' he invited, in a rather high-pitched voice.

Mannering sat in a high, narrow chair, hardly designed for comfort.

'Mr. Marriott,' Saxon went on, 'why are you looking for a position? A man with your stated qualifications should have no difficulty, none at all.'

'I wish to live in London,' Mannering answered, 'and I am not well known here.'

'Family reasons?'

'Personal reasons, Mr. Saxon,' Mannering answered.

'You've got to understand me,' Saxon said. 'The kind of position you seek has very special requirements. You have to *prove* your integrity—could you take out a substantial bond?'

'Yes, of course,' Mannering said. 'If the position justified it.'

'I don't understand you.'

'If I took out a guarantee bond to insure my employer against being robbed by me I would have to approve of my employer,' Mannering said mildly. 'What is sauce for the goose——'

'Yes, yes,' interrupted Saxon. 'I understand. What are your personal reasons for coming back to London. I have to *know*!'

'I am a Londoner by birth,' Mannering replied. 'I've lived abroad most of my life, and now I'd like to come back and settle here.'

'That is the *only* reason?' demanded Saxon.

'Yes,' said Mannering. 'The only reason.'

'I see. I see. According to what you said on the telephone you have a thorough knowledge of and familiarity with *objets d'art*, miniatures, precious stones—all that kind of thing.'

'I have,' Mannering asserted.

'You could prove that, of course.'

'Without difficulty,' Mannering said confidently.

'Have you any objection to travel?'

'Travel where?' asked Mannering.

'Anywhere in the world,' said Saxon, in a lordly way.

'Provided my home base is London, no,' Mannering said. 'I wouldn't want to live abroad, but I've made that clear.'

'I see. I see. What salary would you require?' Saxon demanded, as if he felt sure that at last he had found a question which would make Mannering hesitate.

'Two thousand pounds a year, with all expenses and all housekeeping costs in addition,' stated Mannering without a moment's hesitation.

Saxon leaned back in his chair, his eyes bright with shock. He pursed his lips as if he were going to utter an expletive, and then said in a very shrill voice: 'You realise that is a *very* high salary.'

'It is by English standards, but not by American.'

'You *would* be based in England, remember.'

It was Mannering's turn to pause, and he did so for a long time, then smiled faintly.

'Mr. Saxon, I'm not interested in chicken feed, and I'm an expert. Experts cost money. Do you have a position for me or don't you?'

Saxon did not show any disapproval as he answered:

'I have one for which you might prove suitable. Are you free for an interview this afternoon?'

'Yes. Now or any time.'

'At five o'clock?'

'Yes.'

'In which case,' said Saxon, picking up the receiver of a telephone by his left hand, 'I will speak to Sir Cornelius Vandemeyer at once.'

He shot Mannering a cunning look, as if to see whether

the name meant anything to Mannering, but Mannering showed no more than a casual interest.

That was not easy.

If Vandemeyer was as anxious as this to see a prospective employee, then he was in urgent need—and it made the dismissal of Gillespie an even greater mystery. Saxon dialled a number, had to wait for a long time, and then said with great deference: 'May I speak with Sir Cornelius, please? ... Julian Saxon ... Yes, of *Saxon's* ... Yes, I will hold on.' There was another pause before he spoke again and this time he seemed to spring to attention even as he spoke. '*Good* afternoon, Sir Cornelius. I have an applicant who might—who might *possibly*—be suitable for the position you have vacant ... A Mr. Marriott, John Marriott ... Excellent references, sir, and an excellent background in the—ah—the antiques and *objets* business ... Yes, he is free ... Yes, I *do* have every reason to believe he might be eminently suitable ... Shall I instruct him to come and see you at once? ... *Very* good, Sir Cornelius, he will be there. Thank you very much.'

Saxon rang off, stared at Mannering, pursed his lips, and then spoke with very great precision:

'This is a *wonderful* opportunity, Mr. Marriott. Quite remarkable. I advise you to act with great circumspection with Sir Cornelius. Susan!' He peered at the door and it opened at once. 'Susan, dear,' said Julian Saxon, 'make out a card of introduction for Mr. John Marriott to Sir Cornelius Vandemeyer, if you please.'

CHAPTER 8

SIR CORNELIUS

THE girl Susan smiled up at Mannering and said in warm undertones: 'I do hope you get it.' He smiled back in pleased surprise as he went out. The hair-cord carpet on the steep stairs was a worn wine-red, and he nearly tripped on the bottom bend, where there was a ragged hole.

'Steady,' he warned himself.

He had just time to walk to Ellesmere Square, and it was good practice to walk with a rather loping stride, very different from his natural one. As he turned into the Square his heart beat faster, and he was nearer a mood of real excitement than he had been for a long time.

He must be doubly careful.

He scanned the porticoed Georgian houses, noting that the numbers were painted in black on white pillars. Number 17 was in the middle of one side, with a balcony over the porch from which scarlet geraniums, vivid in the early evening light, hung as bright as dayglo posters. Mannering, approaching from Ellesmere Street, entered the Square from the opposite side of the road. He glanced towards Number 17, not attempting to hide his interest.

A man stood on the balcony, only half-hidden by the deeper shadows, probably since he was out of sight.

Why should anyone stand there except to watch him?

Mannering felt his heart thumping almost suffocatingly, but it did not make him pause or change his gait.

He crossed the road between a taxi and a mini-car, and went along by the railings which guarded the garden in the middle of the square. Here there were tarmac paths, well-kept grass, laurel and rhododendron bushes, a bed or two of late tulips all, now, a little drooping. Only two dogs and a couple of children were within the garden itself.

Mannering, acutely conscious of the man above, stepped on to the porch of Number 17 and rang the bell. The door was a polished black, with a brass bell on one side, and an imposing brass knocker.

A youthful, sparsely haired man opened the door.

'I've an appointment with Sir Cornelius Vandemeyer,' Mannering said.

'What name, sir, please?'

'John Marriott.' He must be extraordinarily careful in saying 'Marriott', a split second of self-consciousness or over-emphasis might betray him.

'Will you come in please?' The footman stepped aside, and Mannering went in, telling himself that one thing was certain: this was a trained footman. 'If you will wait I will tell Sir Cornelius that you are here.'

'Thank you,' Mannering said.

The hall was like ten thousand halls of that period in London. High-ceilinged, square, spacious, with a staircase leading straight up to a half-landing, and a passage alongside the staircase. One door led to the right off the hall, two more led off the passage, at the end of which was a closed door.

The footman went upstairs. Mannering heard his footsteps as he reached the top landing, heard him tap.

From here, close at hand, a door creaked but did not open wide. Mannering felt quite sure that he was being watched, but took no notice. He examined the two pictures in the hall, a Rembrandt and a Rubens; he had no doubt at all that each was genuine. On the right was a low table, beautifully polished over the centuries—not remarkable, but very good. The heavy carved chairs, though handsome, were not collector items. Everything here confirmed what he had always heard of Vandemeyer; he was a man of good, but not extravagant, taste except in those things which he collected, for which he had no equal.

The footman came back, briskly.

'Sir Cornelius will see you now, sir.'

'Thank you.'

'Please follow me.'

Mannering obeyed.

In a few seconds he would come face to face with a man whom he had often seen and who knew John Mannering well by sight and reputation. It would be the moment of greatest danger. The footman opened the door and went just inside.

'Mr. John Marriott, sir.'

'Ah yes,' said Vandemeyer. 'Yes.'

He stood up from behind a huge desk which would have dwarfed a large man, and Vandemeyer was quite small. He was immaculately dressed in dark grey, and had a good figure. His regular features reminded Mannering slightly of Bill Bristow. He had plentiful silver grey hair which was brushed straight back from his forehead and managed to give the impression of studied carelessness. Mannering had forgotten how pale his grey eyes were, and how well-shaped his lips.

A chair stood in front of the desk.

'Sit down, Marriott,' Vandemeyer said, motioning to the chair as the door closed.

'Thank you, sir,' said Mannering.

'I understand that you have a wide knowledge of *objets
d'art*. I hope that includes precious stones and a good
knowledge of paintings, particularly of miniatures?'
Vandemeyer wasted no time at all.

'It does indeed, sir.'

'I need a man whose knowledge is really exhaustive,'
stated Vandemeyer.

'So I understand,' Mannering said simply.

Vandemeyer looked past him. 'On the wall behind me
are six miniatures. Can you tell me what period they are,
and by what artists? By all means, examine them closely,'
he added as Mannering half-rose from his chair.

Mannering went close to the miniatures.

He took several minutes to answer, then named five
artists, adding: 'I don't recognise the sixth one—I
imagine it is modern, mounted on an old mount.'

'It is by Sydney Nolan,' Vandemeyer confirmed.

'Then I'm not surprised I didn't recognise it.'

'How would you value it?'

'Perhaps thirty or forty guineas for its novelty value.'

'Then I was ill-advised to pay a hundred guineas,'
Vandemeyer remarked.

'It depends on the circumstances, sir, and how badly
you wanted to buy it.'

'Yes. In the corner cabinet behind you there are several
objets d'art. Will you tell me what you can of them?'
Vandemeyer did not stir from his chair.

Mannering went to the cabinet. Obviously the other
pressed a switch, for lights came on, showing each of the
pieces to best advantage. One was a German figurine of
quite unbelievable beauty, one a carved ivory chessman,
the superb lacework of the carving patterned with gold,
one was a piece of carved jade which looked too fragile to
be touched, one a glass paperweight also of great beauty

of colouring, and the last a miniature golden casket. He used a glass to look at each.

Vandemeyer moved at last, joined him and unlocked the cabinet.

'If you need to handle them, do so.'

'The only one I need to handle I would prefer not to,' Mannering said. His voice was perhaps a little more American than it had been before, deliberately assumed. 'I would hate to touch the jade, but I'm not sure whether it is third or fourth dynasty. The others—a Dresden figurine probably by Weins, about sixteen fifty, a fairly recent chessman, I would say nineteenth century and probably Tibetan, the paperweight is Venetian—didn't Leonardo da Vinci experiment with glass-blowing at one time?—and the casket of course is Cellini.'

The casket and the figurine had both passed through his hands, at Quinns.

Vandemeyer said: 'You ask for two thousand pounds a year.'

'Clear except for taxes,' Mannering emphasised as they went back to the desk.

'So I understand. Your references must be unimpeachable.'

'I will stand by them, sir.'

'Who will you refer me to?'

'The Maharajah of Patuasur, Mr. Hisito Tojo of Kyoto and Senhor Ramon Horlden of Rio de Janeiro, sir. Closer at hand, Mr. Bidelot of Rue St. Honoré, Paris, Lord Mendleson——' He knew that each of these would vouch for him as Marriott if he sent word by cable. There would be no problem.

'That will be enough,' interrupted Vandemeyer. 'When can you start?'

'Do I understand you to be offering me the position,

sir?' They were sitting opposite each other across the desk now.

'I am,' Vandemeyer said simply.

'I'm honoured, sir. But if I could ask one or two questions—?'

'If you mean about hours——'

'Not about hours, I will be at your disposal whenever required. I am much more concerned with my quarters, and a more precise definition of my duties. If I may say so, one employer expected rather more valeting and personal—ah—attention than I had understood at the time of the engagement. I am not a valet, sir, or personal servant.'

Vandemeyer looked at him so searchingly that for a moment Mannering was afraid that something had sparked him to recollection. But at last he smiled faintly, and said:

'I don't want a personal servant, Marriott. I want a man whom I can trust in my collecting and who sees these for what they are—rare and beautiful objects, not simply goods which can be bought and sold at a profit. As for your quarters—I will show you where they are.' He got up, rounded the desk and led Mannering along another passage up a shorter flight of stairs, and into a small suite of rooms. There was a living-room with books, television, two winged armchairs, a portable record-player and a shelf full of records. Next to this was a bedroom with a tiled bathroom and shower leading off. In an alcove between the two rooms was a pantry, with an electric kettle, a hot-plate, cups and saucers; everything necessary for the preparation of a light meal.

'Do you find this satisfactory?' asked Vandemeyer drily.

'I do indeed, sir.'

'Have you any other questions before deciding whether

to come and work with me?' asked Vandemeyer.

Mannering noticed the use of 'with me' instead of 'for me' and was sure that this man would not choose his words carelessly; he was equally sure that Vandemeyer wanted him to say 'yes'. But there was one question which had to be asked, and if he failed to ask it, sooner or later someone would wonder why.

'If I may just ask, how it is such a post became vacant?'

Vandemeyer seemed to freeze.

'We will go downstairs,' he said, and led the way, leaving Mannering convinced that he had after all done the wrong thing. As they reached the head of the stairs a door opened and a girl in her late teens or early twenties appeared. Obviously she was in a hurry, as obviously not in good temper. She slammed the door, strode towards the head of the stairs, and then almost bumped into Mannering.

Mannering drew back. 'I'm so sorry.'

'My fault.' The girl spoke with bad grace, then looked away from him towards Vandemeyer. 'Oh, daddy!' she exclaimed in a fury of exasperation, and pushed past him down the stairs.

Vandemeyer's expression was hurt and pained as he watched her go; in that moment he seemed to become oblivious of Mannering. But he squared his shoulders, and led the way to his study. He sat behind the desk and Mannering stood in front of it, thinking about the girl, wondering what Vandemeyer was going to say.

Vandemeyer looked up at him with those pale, steely grey eyes.

'I expect from everyone who works for me—as I will expect from you—absolute loyalty and absolute obedience. If I don't get it, then the association quickly comes to an end. Is that clearly understood?'

'I certainly understand,' said Mannering with feeling.

'I think you have the qualifications for this position. Do you want it?'

'Yes, sir, very much.'

'When can you start?'

'Whenever you wish, sir. Will tomorrow morning be suitable?'

'Certainly. At twelve noon tomorrow, then.'

'I will be here, sir,' promised Mannering, his heart beginning to beat fast again.

'Good.' Vandemeyer stood up and extended his right hand, then pressed a bell-push. Almost at once the footman appeared.

'Wells,' Vandemeyer said. 'Mr. Marriott will be joining me tomorrow and will go into Gillespie's old quarters. Ask Mrs. Wells to get everything ready.'

'Yes, sir,' said Wells.

As they were going down the stairs, Wells a little ahead of Mannering, Mannering sensed a kind of tension which he had not felt before, as if Wells wished to say something significant to him, but could not quite bring himself to do so. All hope of this was lost, however, by the sudden appearance of the girl rushing through the hall to the front door. Without looking up she went out, closing the door with a snap.

'Who is the young lady?' asked Mannering.

'Miss Judy—Sir Cornelius's daughter,' answered Wells. 'You'll get to know her well enough if you stay here.' He did not enlarge on that cryptic remark, and went on quickly: 'What time will you arrive?'

'Just before noon.'

'If you said "noon" don't make it five minutes past,' Wells advised. 'You will find Sir Cornelius very fussy about time.'

'Thanks for the tip,' Mannering said.

He went out and, after the door closed, stood on the porch for a few moments looking at the garden, watching a young woman making a hash of parking a Morris 1000 in a space large enough for a Bentley. He waited until she had finished manoeuvring, then crossed the road, and turned deliberately and stared back at Number 17, as anyone in similar circumstances might do.

A man—could it be the same one?—was standing in the deeper shadows of the balcony above the porch.

Mannering walked thoughtfully back towards Knightsbridge.

He was only just beginning to realise that he had not only escaped recognition but had got the job. The first hurdles were well past. He turned a corner, and as he did so, a girl sprang out of a doorway towards him. He recognised Judy Vandemeyer.

She stood squarely in front of him.

'Are you Marriott?' she demanded.

'Yes, miss. I believe you are——'

'You'll be a fool if you work for my father,' she said tensely. 'An absolute fool!'

'Say, what *is* this?' demanded Mannering, drawling more than before. 'Do *you* mean you don't want me to? Is that it?'

'I mean exactly what I said,' she asserted. 'You'll be a fool if you work for my father. Gillespie—Gillespie worked for him for thirty *years*, and he got sacked at a moment's notice. I shouldn't think you would last thirty *days*,' she added with withering scorn. 'Take my advice, and don't take the job.'

She turned on her heel and hurried away.

CHAPTER 9

A KIND OF BETRAYAL

As Mannering watched the girl, he recalled her expression the moment before she turned away. She had looked angry, bitter, resentful and startled—yes, startled. As this thought flashed into his mind he saw a man on the other side of the road, hurrying. The girl, near the far corner, glanced over her shoulder, and stared not at Mannering but at the hurrying man.

She disappeared.

The man, small, lean, dressed in a grey/brown suit—my God!

Sunlight fell upon the man as he reached the corner and showed a curious haze of green in the suit before he disappeared. A man dressed in a suit like that had killed Josephine.

Still maintaining his loping stride, Mannering reached the corner of Harrods and the main road as the girl appeared on the far side, near the raised section of the pavement. The man in the grey/brown suit with the haze of green was only a few feet behind her. Quite suddenly, as if realising she could not escape from him, the girl stopped, and swung round; even at this distance it was possible to see the hatred in her expression. It was difficult to see what exactly led up to what followed, but the next moment the man appeared to launch himself at her.

Mannering had never seen a man attack a woman with such venom. Trying to cover her face, Judy backed away but the man tore her hands aside and struck her half-a-dozen blows with the flat of his hand. A passer-by shouted something Mannering could not hear. There was a stream of traffic which made it impossible to get across, and two huge trucks then a red London double-decker bus hid the scene from Mannering's gaze.

At least he had time to think.

If he interrupted, going to the girl's rescue, he would make a friend of her and incur the enmity of the man. He couldn't really help the girl yet, but could undermine his own position.

The bus passed.

On the other side of the street a small crowd had gathered, and a policeman was heading towards it. Mannering turned and walked back the way he had come. It seemed a kind of betrayal, but the time might come when he would be able to make some amends.

He walked with those long, loping strides back to the hotel. Before going up to his room he telephoned Quinns from the prepayment box in the hall, and Rennie answered with obvious relish.

'This is Quinns of Hart Row. Can I help you?'

'Can I help *you*, Brian,' Mannering asked in his normal voice.

'Why, John!' exclaimed Rennie. 'It's good to hear you. And thank you for the offer, but Josh and I are still doing fine. Do *you* want anything?'

'Is there a cable from Lorna yet?' asked Mannering.

'No, not yet,' said Rennie. 'Can I call you any place if it comes? I shall be here for two or three hours yet.'

'I'll call you,' Mannering promised. He told himself it was absurd to be even remotely anxious about Lorna, but he would be until he had heard from her. 'Don't wait for me, in case I'm held up. I——' He heard a voice in the background, paused, then heard Rennie say: 'Yes, it is.

Hold on, John—Josh wants a word with you.'

There was the briefest of pauses.

'Good evening, sir,' said Larraby. 'I obtained one further piece of information late this afternoon which may be of some assistance.'

'What was it?' asked Mannering.

'Before he disappeared, Sir Cornelius's man Gillespie was making some inquiries about recent purchases made by his employer—the implication being that he questioned the genuineness of some of the articles bought. And on two occasions Gillespie had a young woman with him.'

'Who was she?' inquired Mannering.

'The description tallies with that of Sir Cornelius's daughter, Judy.'

'Does it, by jove,' Mannering exclaimed. 'That could be very useful indeed. Thank you, Josh.'

'Is all going well with you, sir?'

'Very well, I think. I want you to cable . . .' He gave the instructions about the references, and explained why they might be taken up.

'I don't really know whether I'm glad to hear it,' said Larraby with characteristic honesty. 'Be very careful sir, won't you?'

'Very careful indeed,' Mannering assured him.

He rang off, frowning. An Indian woman in a green and yellow sari was standing nearby, waiting patiently to use the telephone. As Mannering stepped out, she flashed a smile at him and went in. Soon she was talking very quickly into the mouthpiece. Mannering went into the street. Rush hour was over, no one seemed to be in a hurry, except two drivers of mini-cars who roared towards Fulham. A bus loaded with passengers from the airport turned into the BEA terminal. Mannering's steps hurried with a certain agitation. Lorna wouldn't be out of his thoughts for long until he'd had that cable. He went back to the hotel, passing the pretty Indian girl on his way, and took her place in the telephone box. He dialled Bristow's home number, and Bristow's wife answered.

'No, he's not home yet,' she said. 'I'm expecting him any minute. Can I get him to—oh, hold on! I think I can hear him at the door!'

In a few seconds, Bristow said: 'What is it?'

'It's John Marriott,' Mannering said in his assumed voice.

'Do I know you, Mr. Marriott?'

'I've just followed a certain Mr. Gillespie into a job,' Mannering said.

There was a split second's pause before Bristow said in a much more relaxed voice: 'Oh, have you. I don't know whether to congratulate you or not.'

'You're echoing Josh Larraby,' said Mannering, in his normal speaking voice. 'Any new reason for being nervous, Bill?'

'No,' said Bristow. 'I'm uneasy about it, that's all.'

'Do something else for me, will you?' asked Mannering. 'What is it?'

'Get all the information you can about the relationship between Vandemeyer and his daughter Judy—an attractive nineteen-year-old, I would say.'

'I will,' said Bristow. 'Is there any particular slant?'

'She and Gillespie seemed to have something in common,' Mannering told him. 'Is there any trace of Gillespie?'

'Absolutely none,' Bristow answered, and then added almost ominously: 'Be careful, John.' It was like a refrain.

'I'll be careful,' promised Mannering again.

He was very preoccupied when he rang off.

He was still preoccupied when he ate a steak at a steakhouse at a quarter of the price he would pay in restaurants he normally patronised. He walked back to the hotel and telephoned Quinns again. This time there was no answer, he had left it too late, and Larraby, who lived above the shop, was often out in the evenings. Tonight he was doubtless probing into the Vandemeyer mystery.

At half-past nine next morning when he telephoned Quinns again, Rennie was already there, and a moment later Mannering's spirits rose with a relief, which told him how anxious he had been.

'Yes, there's a cable,' Rennie reported. 'It reads "Perfect flight. New York's as fabulous as ever. Be careful darling, Lorna".' Rennie paused. 'How very strange that she should cable from New York when she's really in Johannesburg! Don't you think so?'

Mannering stepped out of a taxi at four minutes to twelve. The Johannesburg/New York muddle—so inexcusably careless on his part—could have needed a good deal of explaining away with anyone else. Rennie had accepted the explanation 'she wants to avoid press publicity', readily enough—too readily, really, for honest belief. Well, there was nothing more he could do about it now. Mannering turned resolutely towards 17 Ellesmere Square. Wells, immaculate and more deferential than he had been yesterday, took his two suitcases. Mannering followed him up the stairs. Again he was aware of doors opening, of being watched. One door which led into a first-floor room at the front of the house, opened wider and the man who had been so violent with Judy appeared. He stared at Mannering with veiled insolence, standing squarely in his path.

Mannering stopped, and looked down on the man, who now wore a suit of navy blue. He had thin features, a sallow complexion, heavy-lidded bright eyes. There was the shadow of a beard about his chin and mouth, betraying a man who used an electric razor. He did not move.

'May I pass?' asked Mannering politely.

'There's room,' the man answered, and to Mannering's surprise his accent was Cockney, not remotely foreign.

'There isn't room for me,' Mannering said flatly.

'Mr. Marriott,' began Wells, agitated for the first time, 'you ought to——' He broke off, seeing the two men confronting each other and apparently resigning himself to the fact that they would have to resolve the issue between themselves.

It was too late for Mannering to give way now, but the small man was looking as if he meant to stand fast. It could only have been seconds, but it seemed an age before there was an interruption.

The study door opened and Vandemeyer appeared.

Mannering said briskly: 'Good morning, Sir Cornelius.'

'Good morning,' Vandemeyer said. 'Will you come and see me at two o'clock? Wells will tell you what arrangements are made for lunch. Buff, I want to see you at once.'

'Buff' was an unbelievable name for the man who blocked Mannering's path but he answered to it, looking up into Mannering's face with a truculent 'you haven't heard the last of this yet' expression. Then he turned to Vandemeyer and they both moved into the study. Wells, still agitated, led the way up the second flight of stairs.

Mannering's quarters had been cleaned and polished; everything shone. There were fresh towels in the bathroom, newspapers by the side of one of the armchairs. Wells put the two suitcases into the bedroom, then stood back. He looked more human than before, less of an automaton.

'You took my advice about being on time,' he said.

Mannering smiled. 'I always take good advice.'

'I've some more for you,' said Wells. 'Don't cross Buff.'

Mannering didn't respond.

'He's a bad man to cross,' Wells went on. 'Believe me.'

'I can imagine it,' Mannering said. 'I might be a bad man to cross, too. You could pass that on to Buff. Who *is* Buff, by the way?'

'He's Sir Cornelius's personal servant,' answered Wells. He did not make any further reference to Buff or give any other warning, merely stating, as he went off, that a cold lunch would be sent up to Mannering at one o'clock. Mannering unpacked, already positive about one thing. Buff was much more than a personal servant; any man who dared attack his employer's daughter and then get away with it, must have a very tight hold over his employer.

And Vandemeyer was behaving as if he were being blackmailed.

As he worked, Mannering realised it was very quiet up here, the only sound being the hum of distant cars.

He made a thorough search of his apartment and came across books with the name Gillespie on the flyleaf, a comprehensive collection on all branches of the antique, jewel and *objets d'art* business, all well-thumbed. He moved each one and looked behind it, and then searched beneath and behind the bed—and he found the first thing he was looking for: a tiny microphone, built into the wooden head panel. It was so small that only close scrutiny would have revealed it.

He found another beneath the table where the telephone stood, another on top of a cabinet in the kitchen, yet a fourth in the side of a carved oak fireplace. Satisfied there were no more here, he went outside and inspected his landing. There were 'bugs' in the banisters, others at the newel post. He raised a picture on the well-lit landing and found another, went closer to the study and found one behind a bracket on which stood an early Limoges figurine.

His office was thoroughly covered; not a word could be uttered in this house without it being overheard and recorded. It had been installed for a long time, for Gillespie in the apartment, not simply for him.

Who spied on whom?

Vandemeyer on Buff, or Buff on Vandemeyer? Or was there a third person of whom he knew nothing?

Very satisfied with his discoveries, he enjoyed an excellent cold lunch, with coffee as good as it could be. Wells' wife was obviously a good provider.

He was at Vandemeyer's study at one minute to two, tapped, and tried the handle. The door was locked. He stood aside as footsteps sounded down below, and Vandemeyer said:

'Yes, I will be in for dinner, Deirdre.'

'Not for tea?'

'I doubt it,' he said.

'Will Judy be back?'

'I don't know,' Vandemeyer said. 'I really don't know.'

He started up the stairs and Mannering had a foreshortened view of Deirdre—enough to see how attractive she was, not to see her expression. She disappeared into a front room.

'Ah, there you are,' Vandemeyer said to Mannering. He unlocked the study door, preceded Mannering, then locked the door behind him. 'I want to get some things from my safe,' he went on. 'I don't want anyone to come in while we've got them out. Are you settling in comfortably?'

'I think so, sir,' said Mannering.

'Only think so?' Vandemeyer asked sharply.

'Two things have rather troubled me, sir,' said Mannering, 'and I think you should know about them.'

'What are they?' demanded Vandemeyer.

'In the first place, the man whose name, I understand, is Buff, was obstructive and offensive, and I wouldn't like to feel that he would go on behaving like that.'

'How obstructive and how offensive?' demanded Vandemeyer slowly.

'Enough to make me feel acutely unwelcome, sir.'

Slowly, Vandemeyer nodded.

'I see. I will attend to that. What is the other matter?'

Even now Mannering hesitated, and yet he knew that what he was about to say was unavoidable. Vandemeyer may have been told of the two incidents, and if he had, he would expect Mannering to mention them. For a second time he felt as if he were guilty of a kind of betrayal as he answered.

'Soon after I left here yesterday a young lady whom I had seen in this house warned me not to work for you. It was a most unexpected and unwelcome encounter and it made me wonder if there was resentment at my engagement. The encounter with Buff increased that uncertainty, sir. I am fully prepared to give you of my very best, but if I am to be obstructed—I am sure you will understand me, when I say that it might be wiser for me not to start.'

Vandemeyer said: 'I must say you are remarkably frank.'

'It isn't wise to be otherwise, surely.'

'No.' Vandemeyer picked up a pencil and began to play with it. 'I will be equally frank. My daughter regarded Gillespie, your immediate predecessor, as a very close friend. The relationship between them was like uncle and niece. She did and does resent his dismissal, but I have no reason to believe that she will in any way blame you for it. She might well try to prevent *me* from replacing Gillespie.' Vandemeyer gave a rather brittle smile. 'She is a very self-willed young woman. I will speak to her and I don't think she will create further problems.'

'Thank you, Sir Cornelius.'

'As for Buff,' said Vandemeyer, 'he is a valued servant and I find it necessary to make allowance for certain crudities of manner. I've no reason to believe they will become worse. If they should——' Vandemeyer shrugged his shoulders. 'Then we can deal with the situation as it arises. Now! I want you to watch me very closely. The safe here is different from most others, built partly in the wall and partly in the floor. I want you to become familiar with the method of opening and with the contents.'

He got up and moved to the corner cabinet which Mannering had seen yesterday, and touched a spot on one side. The whole cabinet moved out from the wall, revealing what seemed to be bare brick and a square of uncarpeted floor. Vandemeyer touched another button, also in the cabinet, and the wall began to slide sideways, the square of floor to slide beneath the wall, revealing a short flight of steps.

Vandemeyer switched on a light, which spread gradually along a passage-like chamber with shelves on either side. There was just room for men to walk, one at a time. And as the light became stronger, there were a myriad scintillations as if they had suddenly stepped into the heavens and were among the stars.

This was a treasure house the like of which Mannering had never seen.

CHAPTER 10

THE TREASURE HOUSE

MANNERING stood at the foot of the steps, stupefied by what he saw.

On narrow shelves, in illuminated alcoves lined with mirrors, hanging from the shelves themselves, placed on ledges built into the ceiling, were jewels and *objets d'art* of great beauty. And not only was the radiance pristine white in places, there was colour—from rubies and emeralds, pearls and sapphires, from rose-tinted diamonds, from precious and semi-precious stones of such variety. The very walls were encrusted, diamonds almost as large as pigeon's eggs were set in marble or in jade, in silver or in gold.

It was a chamber of light; as if a rainbow had been entrapped.

Mannering did not know how long he stood entranced, absorbing the beauty, his spirit bowed in silent homage.

'So you really love jewels,' Vandemeyer said at last. 'I thought you did, but was not sure.'

Mannering said huskily: 'Love them? They are breath and blood and the reason for living.'

'I know,' said Vandemeyer. 'To me also they hold the significance of life and death.'

His voice was like a whisper and he spoke as if this were a holy place. To some, to him, to Mannering, to Larraby, that was precisely what it was. There were men who would go further and put these wonders not only beyond price but above life.

Very slowly, reluctant to take his eyes off the scintillating brilliance, Mannering turned his head so that he could see Vandemeyer a few steps behind him. The man's thin face was transformed, he might have been a priest who had seen visions. His eyes caught and held the reflections in this chamber of treasure, no longer pale grey but mirrors of colour.

'It is—unbelievable,' Mannering murmured.

'It is a life's work,' Vandemeyer answered. 'My life's.' And then in a voice which Mannering only just heard, he went on: 'Part of it, that is.'

'Part of——' began Mannering, but the words died away in his throat.

'Stretch up and press the signet ring set above your head,' ordered Vandemeyer. 'Press it a little away from you.'

The ring, which must have been made for and worn by princes, was set in black marble which enhanced even its magnificence. Mannering hesitated. Used though he was to precious stones he knew moments, in such moods as this, when it seemed sacrilege to touch some gem which he had never seen before. He first put his forefinger in it, lightly, then pressed as he was told; as his pressure increased the wall across the passage, perhaps five feet away, slid to one side. Other lights beyond shone into a second chamber, in its way as magnificent as this.

Here were religious jewels; ikons; bishop's crooks and golden eagles, placed on shelves and in alcoves as in the other room, but all of them larger, so that there were fewer pieces. Mannering saw *objets* from the altars and the chapels of Christendom, of Roman Catholic, Russian and Greek Orothodox churches, jewel-encrusted insignia from the religions of the world. He saw rings and amulets from the tombs of the Pharaohs, relics from the Aztec and the Mayan temples, idols, and statues of sacred Hindu animals and priests.

Vandemeyer said: 'Can you bear to see more?'

'*Can* there be more?'

'Press the base of the golden goblet on your right,' instructed Vandemeyer.

The goblet was of wrought gold of such delicacy that it seemed a risk to place a finger on it, but Mannering pressed, warned this time what to expect. And as another door silently opened, still more lights went on in the third chamber in this buried treasure house, and here were *objets* of greater variety, carved from gold and wrought from silver, strange figures made of ivory, jade and amber, of rare woods brought from all the corners of the ancient world. Mannering paced slowly along, looking right and left and marvelling.

'I truly believe it is the most magnificent collection in the world,' said Vandemeyer.

'I have never seen——' began Mannering, and then caught his breath. In his mind was the fact that he had seen most of the world's collections, whether privately or publicly owned, and except for one place he had seen nothing to approach the magnificence here: the Vatican. But 'John Marriott' would not have seen a tenth as much and for a moment he was thinking as Mannering, the owner of Quinns.

There was ever-present danger that he would make a mistake which could betray him.

Another warning ticked in his mind but did not take shape. It was a sense of uneasiness, that there was something here he did not understand. He watched the colours fade from Vandemeyer's eyes as his new employer joined him, and said:

'Will you lead the way back? I will put out the lights.'

Mannering walked with great deliberation. Darkness fell behind him as the doors closed silently. At last he climbed into the study and walked towards the big, leather-topped desk. He felt a sense of apprehension, but there was no apparent cause. Vandemeyer pressed a button on the side of the corner cabinet which slipped back into position.

'Do you see how that was done?' he asked.

'The false wall, you mean.'

'Yes,' said Vandemeyer. 'When I had this house modernised nearly twenty years ago, this room was given two false walls—and the chambers were installed—for the safe-keeping of documents, you understand. The world had experienced wars, destruction and revolutions enough to find this safeguard reasonable.'

'I see,' Mannering said. 'Who made the shelves and the alcoves, and installed the machinery?'

'Gillespie,' answered Vandemeyer. 'He is a fine craftsman.'

Mannering felt, on that instant, that Gillespie was dead. No man in his senses would dismiss a servant who knew everything there was to know about such a treasure house. He would know that Gillespie would have a dozen eager markets for his information and for his intimate knowledge of the 'safe'. Such a man either had to be on one's side—or dead.

Was he letting his imagination run riot?

Vandemeyer sat at his desk; he had not spoken again. Mannering, too, sat down, feeling as if he had run a long way. He must not appear to be a fool, yet mustn't be too obviously curious.

'I couldn't put up that kind of installation,' he stated.

'You won't be expected to,' Vandemeyer assured him.

'What precisely are my duties, sir?'

'To catalogue, value and keep in perfect condition all the things you have just seen,' said Vandemeyer. 'To study catalogues of sales, to attend auctions, particularly at Christie's and Sotheby's. And in general,' he added drily, 'to make yourself invaluable to me.'

'As Gillespie did,' Mannering almost retorted, but he stifled the impulse.

'I can imagine nothing I would like better,' he answered. 'Do I understand that there is no catalogue in existence?'

'There is one which is incomplete and unreliable,' answered Vandemeyer. 'I want you to begin as if from scratch. There's one thing I must make clear, and which I am sure you will understand.'

'What is that?'

'You will only be allowed to work in the vault when I am up here and the door is locked.'

'I understand.' Mannering got up and went to the windows, examining them closely. 'Toughened?' he asked.

'Bullet-proof,' Vandemeyer said. 'This room is quite impregnable, Marriott. There are burglar-proof devices of the most up to date kind. No one can possibly break in—or out,' he added grimly. 'I have taken every conceivable precaution. Now! You will need books, ledgers, other stationery and no doubt a card index system. I will be guided by you. Order what you want and have it invoiced to me. How long do you think it will take to get what you need?'

'I can tell you better after I've been to Harrods,' Mannering said. 'I'd like to go there this afternoon.'

'The sooner the better,' Vandemeyer acquiesced.

Twenty minutes later Mannering went out, still bemused and dazzled by what he had seen, puzzled by some of the implications. Walking to Harrods, he noticed a man leaving a house nearly opposite Number 17. He noticed the same man in both the stationery and the office equipment department. Going back to Vandemeyer's house, he saw him again.

He had no doubt at all that he had been followed; it was obvious that Vandemeyer was not taking him on trust. He would be followed everywhere.

Each time Mannering went out in the next two days, he was followed.

Twice it was by the man whom he had first seen; twice, by a middle-aged woman who wore different clothes each time; once, by Buff.

They knew every step he took.

There was no chance at all of going to a telephone unobserved, of making a purchase anywhere, of meeting Larraby, the police or anyone from Quinns. And for those first two days he made no attempt to evade his followers, simply made sure he would recognise them all again. The equipment he needed was delivered, and he was given the use of a small room across the landing from the study in which to keep the records. Vandemeyer twice took him into the strong-room, then allowed him to find his own way in. He made three mistakes at his first attempt, only one at the second, and thereafter, none.

On the third day, he began his cataloguing.

And on the afternoon of the fourth day, he saw Judy again.

She was standing on the landing when he was coming down from his apartment. Her eyes were shadowed and she seemed to be in real distress. He stopped, without speaking.

'I must see you,' she whispered.

'Miss Judy, really——'

'Tonight. In your apartment, eleven-thirty,' she whispered, and without another word, she sped down the main stairs. Almost at the same time, Buff appeared from the room which led to the balcony.

'Who was that?' he demanded.

'Miss Judy, I think,' Mannering said.

'Either you know or you don't. Who was it?'

'Mr. Buff,' Mannering said very quietly, 'either you know how to speak to me or you don't. If you speak to me like that very often, I will——'

'Don't tell me,' sneered Buff. 'You'll tell the Boss.'

'Oh no,' said Mannering. 'I wouldn't worry him with a trifle. I will simply break your neck.'

He turned on his heel and went into his office room. It would not have surprised him had Buff followed, but the door did not open and when he went out at the summons from Vandemeyer, the little Cockney who looked like an Italian was nowhere in sight.

Vandemeyer wanted nothing special, only a report on progress, and Mannering spent two hours alone in the strong-room. It was nearly five o'clock when Vandemeyer summoned him again by ringing a bell.

'I am going out early and won't be back until late,' he said. 'You haven't asked for any time off yet, Marriott.'

'I would like this evening, sir.'

'Then take it. This isn't a prison, you know.'

'It—it's like a cage of light,' Mannering said in a subdued tone. 'But I must get in touch with one or two distant relatives, and people to whom I have introductions. They won't encroach on my duties, I assure you.'

'I'm sure they won't,' Vandemeyer said drily.

Mannering went out just after six o'clock, and this time the woman followed him. He passed Judy at the wheel of a Sunbeam Talbot, and she nodded distantly.

He stepped into a public call box and telephoned Quinns, hoping that Larraby would answer; and it was Larraby.

'Josh, I've only a moment,' Mannering said quickly. 'Tell Bristow everything is going smoothly, that I think Gillespie is dead, that the daughter Judy is in serious trouble. I'm followed every time I leave the house, but I'll send a description of the three different people who follow me. Have you got all that?'

'Yes, sir,' Larraby said. 'I spoke to Mr. Bristow only an hour ago—he will be as glad as I am to have news of you.'

'Good. Had he any for me?'

'Only negative, sir—he hasn't yet found any trace of Gillespie. There is a letter from Mrs. Mannering, sir. Shall I send it to you anywhere?'

'*Poste Restante*, Knightsbridge,' Mannering said. 'I'll collect it tomorrow. How are things at the shop?'

'Mr. Rennie is a tremendous enthusiast,' said Larraby.

'I gathered he was,' replied Mannering, and rang off remembering that offer of a million pounds for a half-interest in Quinns. He would be a fool not to take it. He stepped out of the kiosk and as he did so, saw his woman trailer moving out of a nearby doorway: Buff and probably Vandemeyer would know he had made a call. He went into the first pub he passed, had a whisky and soda, glanced through the evening papers, and then ordered steak and chips at the bar. By the time he had finished it was half-past seven. He went by bus to Piccadilly and saw a lively Western film at a cinema in the Haymarket.

When he came out he was followed by a man, not the woman.

He went back to Ellesmere Square, and Buff opened the door to his ring. Neither spoke, and Mannering went straight to his rooms. He made coffee, turned on the record-player and listened to Brahms for half-an-hour. It was then nearly half-past eleven, and he wondered if Judy would come.

At a quarter to twelve, he looked out of the apartment but there was no sign of her. As she hadn't come by a quarter past twelve, he decided to turn in. He was in bed with the light out by a quarter to one, and despite the problems pressing on his mind, soon went to sleep.

He had no idea how long he had been asleep when a sound in the room disturbed him.

CHAPTER 11

PLEADING

MANNERING was wide awake on the instant.

He heard a rustle of movement from the door. Was someone simply trying to get in?

No: someone was already in. He heard the door click as it closed. He did not move. Who but Judy would come in here and close the door? Anyone who had come to kill or to rob would leave the door open as a way of escape.

He saw the girl in the pale light of the moon as she tiptoed towards him. He had a fleeting impression that she was used to doing this, for she came quickly towards the bed and stood looking down. Only her face was in the light, now. She wore a dark dressing-gown, which hardly showed at all. He thought she was crying. He waited, for if he let her know that he was awake it might both unnerve her and make her suspicious.

At last, she spoke:

'Mr.—Mr. Marriott. Please wake up.'

He did not move.

'Please wake up,' she pleaded a little more loudly, and then stretched out her hand and touched his shoulder.

This time he stirred.

'It's Judy,' she said with quiet urgency. 'It's me, Judy. Please don't make a noise.'

At last he opened his eyes, and began to hitch himself up on his elbows. She drew away, then suddenly began to sob. Once started, she could not stop, just stood there with her hands at her face, crying. He sensed that she was trying to stifle the sound, but this deliberate attempt at restraint only made the paroxysm worse. He pushed back the bedclothes, got out of bed and put his arm round her shoulders, holding her firmly.

He did not speak, just let her cry.

But he was alert for the slightest sound from outside. It was inconceivable that she would be allowed to visit him without being observed, but they might let her talk, then question him, then check his answers with the hidden tape-recorder.

At last, she quietened.

By then he could see the soft light of the moon on her glossy, dark hair, on the side of her face, on her hands. He let her go and moved to the bedside, putting on the lamp there; it shone vividly on the pillow but hardly at all on the rest of the room. He pulled an armchair into position near her, and said:

'Sit down, Judy.'

Very slowly, she sat down, taking her hands from her tear-stained face.

'What has upset you so much?' he asked.

'I'm sorry,' she muttered huskily. 'I shouldn't have come.'

'What made you?' asked Mannering.

'I used to come here often, to see—to see Gillie.'

'You mean Gillespie?'

She nodded.

'You'd known him a long time, hadn't you?'

'All—all my life.'

'And coming to see me here reminded you that he's left,' Mannering said.

'Left,' she echoed bitterly. '*Left*.'

'I don't understand you.'

'He—he's dead,' she said, hopelessly. 'They killed him.'

The little tape-recorder would be going round and-round incessantly, and someone might be listening at this very moment. If he covered the bugs they would know and he would never again be trusted, might put himself in acute danger. Yet he wanted to know all that this girl had to say. He *had* to know.

In that moment he was more concerned with how to handle the situation than with what she had said with such positiveness.

'He—he's dead. They killed him.'

She was staring at him challengingly, expecting him to say she was talking nonsense, was imagining murder. He moved towards the dressing-table and picked up a newspaper and a pencil lying there.

'Can you prove what you say?' he asked, almost casually.

'I *know* they did.'

'But can you prove it?'

'I tell you I know they did. He was afraid they would, he would *never* have left without saying goodbye, or telephoning me. He must be dead.'

Mannering wrote in big letters on the margin of the newspaper:

'Don't say too much.'

He held it out towards her and turned the lamp so that she could read. He put a finger to his lips. She started, opened her mouth but did not utter a word.

Again he asked a question she obviously didn't expect.

'Have you told your father that you think like this?'

'Yes, he—he won't listen.'

'Your mother?'

'My mother is dead.'

'Your stepmother.'

'She—she won't listen, either,' Judy said.

'Have you asked them if they can prove to you that Gillespie is alive?' asked Mannering.

She looked astonished.

'No, I—but if he's dead, they can't prove he's alive!'

'But if they can prove it, then you'll know you've no justification for suspicion,' Mannering said. He was writing on another margin, and she watched the movement of his pencil as he went on: 'I understand that your father found out that Gillespie was untrustworthy, and——'

'It's not true! He would have *died* for Daddy.'

'And that your father, with great reluctance, had to dismiss him. If that were so he would be hesitant to get in touch with you, wouldn't he?'

'Oh, what's the use!' she exclaimed. 'You don't take me seriously. No one does.'

Mannering held out the newspaper as he said:

'I take this very seriously indeed. I can tell that you are acutely distressed and overwrought, and you need absolute assurance. If you can't get it, then it's obviously a matter for the police.'

She was reading: *'Meet Lionel Spencer red sports car Victoria Albert Museum tomorrow 4 p.m. Take this, learn it, destroy it.'*

Her eyes glowed with great brilliance as he tore the marginal strip off quietly, talking over any sound the paper made. She read it again and tucked it down in her dressing-gown pocket.

'You can safely leave this with me, Judy—but I feel sure there is a misunderstanding which can easily be cleared up.'

Her eyes were still bright but her voice was glum and low-pitched as she replied.

'They'll only lie to you. It's no use expecting them to help.'

'Judy!' Mannering said sharply. 'If they prove that Gillespie is alive, will you stop this nonsense?'

'*If* they do,' she said bitterly—and then, entering into the spirit of this deception, she went on: 'Oh, if only they can! If only they can!'

'Excuse me, Sir Cornelius.'

'If it isn't urgent, Marriott, leave this until this afternoon. I have an appointment at eleven-thirty.'

'I think it is extremely urgent and important, sir.'

'Oh, very well.' Vandemeyer sat behind his desk but did not motion Mannering to sit down. He looked tired, nearer the middle-seventies than his admitted middle-sixties. There was a querulous note in his voice, too. He had been out late, of course, but Mannering sensed there was some other cause for his mood. 'Don't beat about the bush. If it is Buff——'

'Your daughter Judy came to my room late last night, sir. She was in a most overwrought state. I understand she visited my predecessor occasionally. She is convinced that he is dead, sir—murdered.' He paused just long enough to allow the statement to take effect on Vandemeyer, to see the mingled incredulity and terror creep into his expression, and then added flatly: 'I thought you should know at once.'

Vandemeyer actually stammered.

'*J-J-Judy* said this?'

'Yes, sir.'

'To—*you?*'

'Yes.'

'I—I knew she was distressed at his dismissal but this—it must have turned her mind!'

'It certainly does appear to be an obsession, sir.'

'Good God!' exclaimed Vandemeyer. 'I would never have believed it possible.

'If you will forgive a suggestion, sir.'

'Go on, Marriott, go on.'

'Once you are able to satisfy her that Gillespie is alive, she might recover quickly and naturally.'

Vandemeyer looked away for a split second, unable in that instant to meet Mannering's eye. Then he braced himself and looked back. He moistened his lips; his expression, every line on his face, that of an old, old man. Yet he strove to assert his authority.

'No doubt. But how do you convince a young woman against her will? I can't produce Gillespie out of a hat.'

'Do you know where he is, sir?'

'I do not, I do know he is *very* lucky not to be in prison.'

'I see, sir. Have you heard from him since he left?'

'There was no occasion to hear.'

'If he should write for something he left behind, sir— or if he sent to Miss Judy but she did not receive the letter——' Mannering broke off. 'She certainly needs some kind of reassurance. And if I may say so, sir'—Mannering paused again, drew in a deep breath as if to say what he had to say needed a great effort—'so do I.'

Vandemeyer tightened his lips and gripped the arms of his chair.

'Do you mean that you take the child's delusion seriously?'

'Seriously enough to hope that you can reassure me, sir,' Mannering said. 'This is a unique job and I should hate to give it up, but——'

'You won't have to give it up,' said Vandemeyer gruffly. A new expression in his eyes told Mannering that now the shock was over, he had seen a way out of this dilemma. 'I think I can find where Gillespie is and have him telephone or write to Judy. I had no idea that she felt so deeply.'

'It would be a great relief to hear from him, I'm sure.'

'Yes. All right, Marriott.' Vandemeyer hesitated as if groping for something else to say, and then with obvious insincerity, asked: 'How did your own affairs go last night?'

'I telephoned a cousin, sir, and am to telephone again today to arrange a meeting.' Mannering spoke perfunctorily. 'I'm not wholly satisfied with the coding labels—I would like to go to a firm of library stationers in the City to see if they have something more satisfactory. I propose to place a very small self-adhesive label on the base of every stand, or on each of the exhibits, and——'

'Use your own judgment,' Vandemeyer said, with a return of impatience.

'I will—thank you.' Mannering went out, and as he closed the door he saw Vandemeyer's hand move towards a bell-push. Mannering went across to his own office, closed the door and then opened it a crack. Almost at once Buff appeared from his room—the room off which the balcony led—and went into the study. Mannering heard the key turn in the lock, stepped outside, and pressed his ear close to the door. He heard Vandemeyer shouting, as if the self-control he had shown with Mannering had broken. Mannering heard the words quite distinctly.

'Why wasn't I told? Either you knew she had gone to see him, or you didn't.'

'I knew all right——' Buff began.

'Then why in heaven's name didn't you tell me?'

'Because you came in late and got up late,' Buff answered. He did not sound at all excited. 'You know what you ought to do, don't you?'

'What do you mean?'

'You ought to send Judy away for a few weeks.'

'I've told you before——' Vandemeyer began.

'Now I'll tell you,' said Buff in a matter-of-fact voice. You send her away. She needs a rest, and the longer she stays here the more nuisance she'll be.'

'There will be no need if Judy is reassured,' said Vandemeyer. 'We need a letter, signed by Gillespie. There should be no difficulty about that. Arrange it, Buff—and don't argue. Don't drive me too far.'

'I won't drive you any further than I have to,' Buff said. There was the familiar note of insolence in his voice, which grew louder.

Mannering drew back and stepped across to his own room. He had just time to close the door before the study door was unlocked and opened. Buff's footsteps sounded clearly in the passage.

Mannering went back to his desk, and sat down. No one came to see him.

He left just after three o'clock, and was followed by the middle-aged man again. He went to a stationer's in Chancery Lane, was there for ten minutes, then went into a telephone kiosk, dialled Quinns, and was answered by Lionel Spencer in his rather affected voice.

'Lionel, listen very carefully,' Mannering said. 'Go in your own car to the Victoria and Albert Museum. You'll find a girl, Judy Vandemeyer, waiting there—about five feet four, raven black hair, good complexion. Take her for a drive, make sure you shake off anyone who follows, and then make her talk. You won't find it difficult, she's living on her nerves. Have you got all that?'

'Yes, sir!'

'Don't give her any clue as to who you are or who I am,'

ordered Mannering. 'Say that we are both working for an
insurance company, tracing certain stolen jewels. I think
we can trust her, she hates the set-up so much, and she is
convinced that the man whose place I have taken was
murdered.'

'Is she, by God!' exclaimed Spencer.

'And she's almost certainly right,' said Mannering.
'When you have her story, give a written account of it to
Larraby and tell him to use his judgment about letting
the police know. Is everything clear?'

'Absolutely clear,' Spencer assured him with suppressed
excitement. 'This is a chance in a million, I wouldn't miss
it for the world!'

'Lionel,' said Mannering. 'Listen to me.'

'Yes, sir.' Spencer quickly sobered.

'At least one, possibly two, murders have been com-
mitted in this affair. It isn't even remotely related to a
gay adventure. And Judy Vandemeyer could be in acute
danger. Don't let yourself be followed when you're driving away with her. Is that clearly understood?'

'Very clearly, sir,' said Spencer.

CHAPTER 12

EAGER YOUNG MAN

LIONEL SPENCER put down the telephone and stood absolutely still for at least ten seconds. Then he sprang into the air, holding both hands aloft, and let out a stifled: 'Yip-yip-yippee!'

Larraby, appearing from behind the partition at the back of the shop, had an instantaneous, and sobering, effect.

'That was Mr. Mannering, sir,' said Lionel. 'He was in a very great hurry.'

'That I can imagine,' said Larraby, eyeing the young man keenly. 'Did he appear to be perturbed?'

'I wouldn't say that, sir—simply in a hurry. He wants me to meet a young lady outside the Victoria and Albert Museum at four o'clock.'

'What young lady?'

'Judy Vandemeyer,' answered Lionel.

Larraby put a hand on his shoulder.

'Lionel, listen to me. If you are to be of any real use to Mr. Mannering in this or any other case—or in the business for that matter—you must learn to report quickly and succinctly, omitting no matter of importance. What *precisely* did Mr. Mannering say?'

Lionel, abashed, reported the conversation almost verbatim.

'That's better,' Larraby approved. 'Mr. Mannering has told you enough for the time being, and evidently feels that he can rely on you. Don't let him down.'

In a surge of feeling, Lionel said: 'Don't worry, Josh—
I'll never do that.'

A few minutes later, at the wheel of his sports car, he
realised that he had never before called Larraby 'Josh' to
his face. He went red, and yet he glowed with satisfac-
tion, for Larraby obviously meant it when he said Mannering relied on him.

It was half-past three. Usually he would have reached
the Victoria and Albert in fifteen minutes but the traffic
in Oxford Street was chaotic, and when at last he turned
into Park Lane, a collision between a post office van and
a bus held up traffic for ten minutes. Spencer sat fuming.

He was beginning to fear that he would be late for
Judy Vandemeyer; late on his first assignment! He had
a wild idea of leaving the car and going by foot, thought
better of it, and was fiercely relieved when traffic started
to move again. There was a little carriageway outside the
big, dark building of the Museum which looked like a
cross between a cathedral and a prison, and although
there was no room to park there was room to stand.

Walking up and down outside the museum was a girl
in a green linen suit.

Even had he not been expecting to meet a raven-haired
beauty, this girl would have attracted his attention.
There was something in the way she walked, in her car-
riage, which singled her out. As he got out of the car she
turned, and obviously the red sports car meant something to her for she came hurrying—eager and quite
lovely. Disturbingly lovely. And her hair *was* black as a
raven's wing.

'Miss Vandemeyer?'

'Oh yes. *Are* you—is it you I'm to meet?'

'Yes, indeed,' said Spencer. 'My name is Spencer, Lionel
Spencer. I'm from——'

'There's a man following me,' she said, breathlessly.

'*What?*'

'I'm always followed. I tried to get away but he followed my bus.'

'I'll soon deal with *him*,' declared Lionel Spencer confidently. 'Where is he?'

'Be—careful!'

'Perhaps *he* ought to be careful.'

'No,' she said entreatingly. 'Please don't cause any trouble. Just—just get away from him.'

'All right,' Lionel promised. 'But which one is he?'

'Don't look round,' she said. 'It's the man on the motor-scooter.'

'I'll see him in a minute,' said Spencer. 'And we'll soon get rid of him.'

She rested a hand on his arm and said in a helpless kind of way: 'You don't know them at all, or the impossibility of getting rid of them. I—I even gave up seeing friends because I was always being watched. I hardly know why I've come, the whole thing was hopeless from the start.'

Lionel recalled Mannering's warning that Judy Vandemeyer was living on her nerves; and words and empty promises would give her no reassurance. He took her arm firmly, turned round and guided her to the car, seeing the man on the motor-scooter not thirty yards along the road. He opened the passenger door, smiling broadly at Judy, and saying:

'He's not to know I'm not just another boy-friend.'

'When I'm back they'll want to know who you are, where I met you, why I came out today.'

'Then we'll have to cook up a convincing story,' replied Spencer. 'How about a spin as far as Wimbledon Common? Go a bit farther, if you like.' He got in beside her

and started the engine; the man on the motor-scooter had
already started his, and moved out after Spencer, who
could see him in the driving-mirror. He was a small, wiry-
looking man in a sports jacket and grey trousers, and he
wore a tight-fitting cap. Lionel turned off at Earl's Court
Road, where heavy and fast traffic was going one way,
with the scooter only three or four cars' lengths behind.
He pulled over to the left inside lane and all other traffic
except the scooter roared past. The rider made no
attempt to hide what he was doing.

'Hold tight,' Lionel said quietly.

Judy stiffened: 'What are you going to do?'

'Just hold tight. Ready?' He jamed on the brakes and
the car jolted to a standstill. The motor-scooterist swung
his wheel wildly, just got by, but nearly lost control of his
machine. A huge truck, thundering down, passed within
a foot of him. The scooter engine cut out and the rider
came to a standstill a few feet ahead of the sports car.

'Sit tight,' Lionel urged again. He placed a hand firmly
on Judy's knee, then climbed over the side of the car and
reached the scooterist in a couple of long strides.

'You all right?' he asked in a loud clear voice.

'No thanks to you, you could have killed me.'

'And that's what I shall probably do if you don't get off
my trail,' said Lionel in a voiçe which only just carried to
Judy's ears. 'If I want to take a girl friend out for an hour
or two I don't want a chaperone breathing down my
neck. Understand?'

'You don't know what you're asking for,' the man said
savagely. His face was badly pitted from small-pox, his
eyes were deep-set and an opaque brown. 'Take her back
now, or——'

'Did you ever try driving one of these with part of it
missing?' inquired Lionel. He held the man off with one

hand and pulled up the cover of the engine, loosened the distributor-head and tossed it into a garden opposite. 'I'll take Miss Vandemeyer back when she's ready, not before.'

He let the man go, and swung round. The man lost his balance and struggled to regain it, as Lionel climbed into the driving seat again, kissed Judy lightly on the cheek, and started off. The scooterist glared furiously after them.

'There's a man who would like to cut my throat,' said Lionel.

'You shouldn't have done that,' Judy almost gasped, but she was looking at Lionel with admiration in her eyes. 'He might——'

'Forget him, Judy,' said Lionel as he drove into the stream of traffic. 'Tell me what it's all about. I'm in insurance, and my company's after some jewels which were stolen last week. I work with an insurance investigator, John Marriott. He——'

Judy exclaimed: 'You mean Marriott's a *detective*?'

'In a way, yes, and a damned good one,' said Lionel cheerfully. 'He——'

Judy began to laugh; a stifled kind of giggle at first, it grew into helpless laughter. Lionel was too involved with traffic to spare more than a startled glance or two. She leaned back in her seat and surrendered absolutely to the laughter, and as it went on, almost hysterically, he realised that it was a measure of her relief from tension. He put a hand on her knee.

'Steady on, now—take it easy.'

She went on laughing.

'Judy, it can't be as funny as all that!'

'F-f-f-funny!' she gasped, and at least that interrupted the paroxysm. 'It—it's more than funny—it's hilarious! A detective—Daddy's employed a detective. Oh, it's gorgeous!'

'I know a little place by the river at Richmond where we could have some tea and you can tell me all about it,' Lionel said. 'Will you come?'

'Yes, I'd love to.' Judy tossed her head and raised her hair with both her hands, sitting back and letting the wind carry it streaming behind her. For a quarter of an hour she said hardly a word but seemed to revel in the speed and the wind and the freedom. But when they reached the little inn by the river, not far from the bridge which spanned both river and the centuries, she was subdued again and the glow had faded from her eyes.

It was warm enough for them to want shade from the sun and they had scones and cream and strawberry jam overlooking the fast-flowing Thames. At last she began to talk, quietly and with welcome clarity.

'I'm still not sure whether I ought to tell you,' she said, 'but I couldn't go on as I was—*something* has to be done. You—you don't have to go to the police, do you?'

'No,' he answered, confident that Mannering would agree. 'But perhaps *you* should.'

'I can't,' she said simply. 'I don't know what's going on. I only know that my step-mother went away for some kind of health-course and another woman came back in her place.'

'Good Lord!' exclaimed Lionel. 'That was pretty cold-blooded.'

'Oh, I don't mean Daddy turned her out!' exclaimed Judy. 'I mean someone who looked like my step-mother, dressed like her, *impersonated* her—and Daddy accepted it as if nothing was wrong. I could hardly believe it. I tried to talk to him about it but he only said that Deirdre had been away for this health-course, and she had lost a lot of weight, but it wasn't true, and he knew it.'

'What an incredible story,' said Lionel, meaning it absolutely. He spread more cream on a scone and ate without speaking for a moment, while Judy stared over the river, a film of tears in her eyes. 'What could possibly make him——'

'He's being blackmailed,' Judy said abruptly. 'I believe my stepmother was kidnapped, and he's terrified in case she will be killed. He—he absolutely worships her. He really does. He wouldn't put up with the awful things that are going on if it weren't for that.'

'What awful things?' asked Lionel, gently.

'Well—these men, following us everywhere. A man named Buff who actually runs the house. Daddy's terrified of him. And—there's Gillespie.' She closed her eyes as if in her mind's eye she were seeing something she hated to see. 'He realised something was terribly wrong, that Daddy was being blackmailed, and talked to Daddy about it, and—Daddy told him to leave. He'd worked for Daddy for over thirty years, and he was fired just like that. Only—I don't believe he simply walked out. I believe he would have told me, if he were going. I think Buff killed him.'

'Killed,' echoed Lionel, heavily.

'Oh, I can't be sure, but I feel sure,' Judy declared. 'First Deirdre disappeared, then Gillespie; Daddy is afraid of his own shadow. I'm watched and followed wherever I go.' She turned to Lionel and held her hands out to him; and he gripped them. 'What am I to do? Please tell me. What am I to do?'

'Keep your head, and do whatever John Marriott tells you,' advised Lionel with quiet vehemence. 'When you get back, tell this man Buff or anyone who questions you that I'm an old boy-friend, very quick-tempered, who simply took the man on the scooter to be one of those pests who follow pretty girls.'

'But they'll want to know when I made the date with you and what I told you,' said Judy, half-ruefully.

'Tell them I spotted you by chance outside the Museum, and that you had no intention of discussing your father with anyone,' said Lionel. 'You can bluff that out, can't you?'

'I—yes, I suppose so.'

'And above all, remember to do what John Marriott tells you,' insisted Lionel. 'He's very good.'

'But why did he take on this job? Does he think Daddy knows something about these stolen jewels? Is that what it's all about?'

'That's what we're going to find out,' Lionel assured her. 'Judy——'

'Yes?'

'If it weren't for this dreadful spot you're in I would have enjoyed this tremendously.'

'I—I *have* enjoyed it, in a funny way,' Judy said. 'I don't feel alone any more. And if Mr. Marriott's living at Number 17 it won't be anything like so bad. Unless— unless they discover who he is and what he's doing.' Fear clutched her again, and nothing Lionel could say really reassured her.

CHAPTER 13

FAMILY QUARREL

MANNERING felt completely cut off from Quinns and the outside world when he returned to 17 Ellesmere Square. The front door *was* like the door of a prison, despite the remark Vandemeyer had made earlier. He went to his office, expecting to find an instruction from Vandemeyer but there was none. The office was plainly furnished with bookcases and filing cabinets, a pedestal desk and a large table on which exhibits and cards could be spread freely. The outlook from the window was identical with the one from his bedroom, immediately above.

He was familiar now with most of the routine and knew all the servants of the house.

Apart from Wells the footman and his wife Irene, who was Lady Vandemeyer's personal maid and chambermaid combined, there was a male cook, two middle-aged women who shared most of the household duties, and Buff. All of these lived in, but only the Vandemeyers themselves, Buff and Mannering lived in the main part of the house. The others shared the back which was approached by a second staircase. Here there was a communal living-room and dining-room used exclusively for the staff.

The entire staff was new, yet Mannering had a feeling that Buff, the Wellses and the cook, a stocky north-countryman, were old associates.

He had learned, also, that the men and the woman who followed him lived in a house opposite.

Moving about in the course of his duties, Mannering also learned the lay-out of Number 17 thoroughly in the first four days, by which time everyone was used to him. Even Buff would nod good morning, and no longer went out of his way to be hostile.

Twice, Mannering had heard Lady Vandemeyer's voice, but he had not seen her in the whole of those four days. He concentrated on studying all the others, their movements, their mannerisms, listening to their voices, their accents. Now he was able to judge whether Vandemeyer was at home; there was a noticeable relaxation of discipline when he was out. Mannering tried to imagine what he would feel if he had simply taken the job here, without any fore-knowledge of mystery. Except for Judy's visit there would have been nothing to arouse suspicion.

On that fourth evening, he was very much on edge for Judy's return.

He saw her about half-past six, coming in at the front door. She went straight up to her own room, apparently quite normal. Vandemeyer and his wife were in, the cook was preparing roast duck and green peas, Mannering was expecting to eat downstairs with the staff. At half-past seven there was a tap at his door.

'Come in,' he called, and Judy opened the door.

He could see how excited she was; for the first time since he had known her she seemed free from a weight of anxiety and depression—but she simply put her finger to her lips, and then said:

'My father would like you to join us for a drink before dinner, Mr. Marriott.'

'That's very nice of him. May I come down in two or three minutes?'

'Yes, I'll tell him,' she said—and drew closer to Mannering instead of going out, gripped his arms, stood on tip-toe and kissed him on the cheek. Then she turned and hurried away.

Mannering found himself smiling.

Wells came forward as he went downstairs.

'You're expected, Mr. Marriott,' he said, and opened the second door opposite the stairs.

Mannering had not been in here—or in any of the main ground floor rooms—before. This was a kind of anteroom, with folding doors at either end. One set was open and he saw the dining-room beyond; the other no doubt led to the drawing-room. This was a pleasant, Regency-style room with considerable character.

Lady Vandemeyer—or the woman passing herself off as Lady Vandemeyer—was sitting near the big fireplace. Vandemeyer was standing by an open cabinet where bottles glistened, Judy was sitting at a baby grand piano, playing a little melody which Mannering only vaguely remembered.

'Ah, Marriott,' said Vandemeyer. 'I'm glad you could come.' As if it had not been a command. 'Deirdre darling, you've probably seen Mr. Marriott about—and you've met Judy, Marriott.' No one could have sounded more unperturbed.

'Lady Vandemeyer,' Mannering nodded.

'How are you, Mr. Marriott.'

'What will you have, Marriott?'

'Yes,' Judy said, coming forward. 'Mr. Marriott was very understanding, Daddy.' She came up and shook hands, gravely, and went on without a change in her voice or her expression. 'I'm sorry I was so silly, Mr. Marriott.'

'You were very worried,' Mannering said.

'Judy dear, Mr. Marriott wants a drink,' Lady Vandemeyer interposed.

'Yes. What is it to be, Marriott?' Vandemeyer asked mechanically.

'A whisky and soda, please.'

'Ice?'

'Yes, please—but not on the rocks.'

'We've heard from Gillespie,' Judy announced simply.

Inwardly, Mannering was astounded; outwardly, he showed no sign at all of surprise. 'I'm very glad indeed.'

'He telephoned this evening—not half-an-hour ago,' Judy went on. 'It was such a relief to speak to him.'

'I'm sure it was.'

'Judy has told us how considerate you were,' Lady Vandemeyer said. 'We were most grateful.'

Mannering said: 'Nerves can be very upsetting ... Thank you, sir.'

'To a long and successful association,' Vandemeyer toasted.

Mannering thought: It's too smooth, it's phoney. Judy's happy, but why are the others putting on an act? He drank. 'I'll certainly go along with that!' He turned to Lady Vandemeyer and saw how young she was. The wife whom Lorna had known so much better than Mannering had been in her early forties, but this woman was in her thirties—though made-up to look older, and dressed in the less extreme fashion of the not-so-young. There was, Mannering thought, something artificial about her smile.

'I do hope you will enjoy working here, Mr. Marriott.'

'I'm sure I shall,' answered Mannering, smiling conventionally.

'Marriott's a genuine enthusiast,' Vandemeyer said, joining them. 'A lot of experts can value gems, but very few valuers love them.'

'I'm so sorry we can't ask you to stay for dinner, Mr.

Marriott, we have an urgent appointment.'

Small talk, not too blatantly flattering; Mannering saw in it a cleverly concealed attempt to reassure him—and if he were simply a new employee, it would have succeeded. He took his leave, with murmurs of excessive politeness on both sides.

'Goodnight—goodnight.'

Judy stepped to the door with him, and as he went out, breathed: 'Thank you, oh thank you!' Her eyes were glistening. The Vandemeyers might believe it was because she was reassured over Gillespie but it was excitement after talking to Lionel Spencer.

As he went upstairs, Mannering was tormented by the conviction that there had been undercurrents which he could not understand, undercurrents to fear. What could be their cause?

Buff's surly demand to send Judy away?

Judy's escape from whoever had followed her—alarming Buff and those with him even more?

Mannering went into his room and switched on the television, standing and looking down on it, thinking only of the problem. *Judy,* coming to his room and telling him of her fears, *Judy* escaping their surveillance, *Judy* putting on a show of being satisfied. Had she really fooled them?

There was an urgent domestic matter to discuss.

Judy——

He turned the television loudly enough for it to be heard outside his suite and went downstairs again, making no attempt to conceal himself until he reached the passage leading to the communal staffroom. Wells and his wife were talking ... Buff said something quite funny and they all laughed. The cook and the two women would be in the kitchen.

He went to the room where he had met the Vande-meyers. The sliding doors by the dining-room were partly closed. He went through, safe from observation from the dining-room. One of the others might catch him here but he would find an excuse.

Vandemeyer was saying: 'Judy, I want you to go away for a few weeks. You need a rest.'

'Want me to go *away*!' gasped Judy. 'But I don't want to go away!'

'And I don't want any more arguments,' her father said briskly.

'But, Daddy, it's crazy! If this is just because I wouldn't tell you where I was this afternoon—oh, it's crazy! I've every right to go out with a boy-friend for a few hours, you wouldn't have dreamed of questioning me a few weeks ago!'

'But I do question you now.'

'You've no *right* to! For goodness sake, see *reason*.' There was a few moments of silence, then she cried: 'What on earth's happened to this house? It isn't the same place, it's full of strangers and secrets. It's horrible!'

'Judith!' her father said harshly. 'Stop this nonsense at once.'

'But it isn't nonsense, it's the truth. Everything's changed—even Deirdre's changed!' Judy's voice rose almost to a scream. 'Gillespie said there was something wrong. I don't believe it was him I spoke to. I don't be-lieve——'

There was the sound of a slap—sharp and hard.

Judy gasped.

'Judith,' her father said icily, 'the change in this house-hold is a change in you. You have become quick-tem-pered, suspicious, even shrewish. When you behaved your-self you had the freedom you deserved but you've for-

feited the right to make your own decisions. You are going to spend a few weeks in Cornwall, at the cottage,
and——'

'I won't go away! I absolutely refuse——'

There was another tense silence, and Mannering
sensed that Judy had been shocked to that silence. Then
she gasped:

'No! No, don't let him——'

'Keep still!'

'*No!*' screamed Judy.

It was all Mannering could do to stay where he was,
but if he gave himself away now all his effort would be
wasted, and he could not be sure of doing any good.
There was a gasp, and then Judy muttered:

'You devil. Devil—dev——'

Her voice faded out, and Buff said sharply: 'Don't let
her fall.' There was a flurry of movement, then cutlery
clattered and fell. 'All right, I've got her,' Buff added.
'Before she wakes up from that little lot she'll be in
Cornwall.'

Vandemeyer said in a peculiar voice: 'Don't hurt her.'

'If anyone hurts this baby, it will be the baby herself,'
Buff said. 'Okay, I can carry her.'

Mannering moved swiftly and silently out of the room,
then towards the stairs. The door slammed. There was a
moment of silence before Vandemeyer's voice rose with a
certain anguish. 'I hope to God I've done the right thing.'

Mannering went up to his own room, treading lightly,
left the television on and went to his wardrobe for a scarf
and a short swagger cane with a heavy knob handle. He
left the light on in the sitting-room, turned off the one in
the bedroom and opened the window wide at the bottom.

He climbed out.

There was a drainpipe on his left and almost directly

beneath him the top of the window ledge of his office. He went down quickly, the years rolling back to the days when he would have thought no more of this than going down a flight of steps. Beneath his office was the roof of the back porch. Lights were on at kitchen and scullery. He climbed on to the porch roof and dropped down to the ground.

There were no nearby sounds.

He walked towards the service alley at the end of the garden, into it, and towards Ellesmere Street where it ran into the Square. The porch light of Number 17 was on, and a car pulled up outside. Almost at once the front door opened and Buff appeared, supporting Judy so that she appeared to be walking. The driver of the car got out: he was the middle-aged man who often trailed Mannering. A man was walking a dog farther along the street, but no one else was about. Buff bundled the girl into the back, and began to get in beside her.

Mannering, moving slowly towards the scene on the garden side, pulled the scarf up over his mouth and chin.

He ran ten feet, launched himself at the driver, spun him round and hit him with such force that the man went flying back. Buff, crouching to get into the car, half-turned. Mannering caught him by the leg and pulled him out. And Buff, struggling to get free, slipped and banged his head on the road. He lay stunned. Mannering bent down, tapped his pockets and found a gun in one, took it out and tossed it high into the garden. Buff hadn't stirred. Mannering sprang round to the wheel of the car and got in. The engine was turning sweetly. It was an automatic drive, and he eased the car forward, past the man with the dog, who stood and stared.

Mannering drove out of the Square, into Ellesmere Street, along this towards Knightsbridge. He saw a taxi at stand, pulled up in front of it and jumped out. The driver was reading a newspaper. Mannering thrust a five-pound note through the window.

'My daughter's in the car ahead—dead to the world,' he said. 'Take her home, will you? I've got some unfinished business.' He spoke with savage intensity.

'That's all very well, but——' the man began.

'Twenty-one, Green Street,' Mannering went on. 'Top floor. And whatever you do, don't leave her alone. Twenty-one, Green Street—top floor, remember.'

He turned and hurried back towards Ellesmere Square. Outside Number 17 was a small crowd, including a policeman. He turned into the alley and climbed back into the house the way he had come, stuffing the scarf into his pocket. For the first time he used the telephone; it was a risk, but a very slight one. He dialled Quinns, and Larraby answered from his flat above the shop.

'Josh—about ten minutes from now Judy Vandemeyer should be at my flat. Go there and don't look surprised when you find her in a drugged sleep. A taxi-driver will be with her—I told him Judy is my daughter. Give him a fiver and tell him to forget it. If he insists on calling the police, get in touch with Bristow. Is that all clear?'

'Perfectly,' said Larraby. 'Lionel is with me—we will both go. His report confirms much that you suspect, sir—there are no vital differences.'

'Fine,' said Mannering.

He put down the receiver, and stood quite still. Larraby had taken the instructions as if they were of everyday occurrence. Mannering sat on the arm of a chair and began to laugh silently. He was still laughing when there was a thunderous banging on his entrance door.

CHAPTER 14

LIONEL SPENCER

By the time Larraby had finished talking to Mannering, Lionel Spencer was at the front door of Quinns. His car stood right outside, and he jumped in and started the engine. Rays from a street lamp fell on to the deep red velvet of Quinns window, lighting the two gilded chairs, once the dining-chairs of Belgian princes, which stood there. Lights were left on in the shop by night, and a police patrol passed every fifteen minutes. Lionel knew that, but only respected the extraordinary burglar-proof precautions—the intricate system of alarm and controls which looked simple on the surface but for many years had withstood every attempt to break in.

Larraby came hurrying, and closed the door. He did not need to turn a key in the lock, for every control slipped into place immediately.

Lionel was by the side of the car's open door.

Larraby got into it, nimbly.

'Hold tight!' warned Lionel, as he had warned Judy.

He vaulted into the driving seat and started off with a roar which set sleeping pigeons a-flutter, and made a policeman in New Bond Street turn to stare. Larraby smiled and nodded at him.

'They're a rare box of tricks, they are,' the policeman remarked to himself, and half-smiled and half-frowned as the sports car swung round the corner.

Larraby was clutching the door and the edge of his seat as they turned into Piccadilly, down Bury Street, then into Pall Mall. He cut through to the Mall, where Buckingham Palace stood massive and squat against the pale evening sky.

'We'll be there in ten minutes flat,' boasted Lionel.

'That is presuming we get there at all,' murmured Larraby. 'And Lionel, I'm warning you. Show no surprise at whatever state we may find Judith in.'

'*State?*' growled Lionel. '*State?*' He swung out to pass a cyclist, and then swung round a corner to the left. Lights showed the modern houses, a block of flats, and the tall houses of which Mannering's was one. Outside these was a taxi, unable to get close to the kerb because of parked cars. As Lionel pulled up just behind it, a man came out of a front door and stood looking up and down. Lionel got out and turned towards him.

'Did you bring my sister home?' he called.

'Sister? Who said anything about anyone's sister?' The man was heavily-built and had a big face and an aggressive manner.

'My father told me——' began Lionel, and then he glanced inside the taxi.

Judy sat in a corner, her head lolling on her chest, making no sign of movement. Lionel pulled open the door and leaned in.

'Judy!' he called. 'Judy!'

'Lionel,' said Larraby, swiftly reaching his side, 'there is no need to go into a panic. Lift Judy out of the taxi and take her to the lift.' He took out his wallet, selected a five-pound note, and turned to the taxi-driver. 'Call the police if you think you should,' he went on, 'but make it Scotland Yard and ask for Superintendent Bristow.' He handed over the note—and then for the first time noticed a man on the other side of the road.

He went tense.

Lionel now had Judy cradled in his arms and was turning his back on the taxi. Larraby watched the other man draw nearer, then, in an urgent undertone, called sharply:

'Lionel! Be careful!'

The taxi-driver looked suspiciously from one to the other.

'What's going on here?' demanded the newcomer. He reached the pavement showing no aggressive intent. 'Who are—oh! Josh Larraby!' His voice rose in relief.

'*I* want the police——' began the taxi-driver.

'You've got them,' said the man who had come out of the shadows.

'I'll want proof before I'll believe you,' the taxi-driver growled.

The newcomer took out his wallet and presented a card showing that he was Detective-Officer Wilton of the C.I.D. Though the taxi-driver's suspicions were immediately allayed, dignity demanded that he should not allow himself to be mollified too soon.

'But I still think it's a damned funny business,' he grumbled. 'A man asks me to bring an unconscious girl . . .'

By the time he had told his story, Lionel had taken Judy to the lift and upstairs to Mannering's flat. There was a chair by the lift and he placed her in this carefully, then stood back and looked at her. Now her head lolled to one side and she might well be in a drugged sleep. He bent forward and felt for her pulse. It was beating steadily. Thankfully he stepped back as the lift arrived again and Larraby stepped out.

'They're both satisfied,' he announced, opening the door with a key. 'Shall I help you carry her?'

'No, thanks,' Lionel picked her up more easily this

time, and took her into the flat. Larraby put on lights and led the way into the small spare bedroom and turned down the bed. Lionel put the girl on this carefully.

'Ought we to take off her shoes and loosen her clothes?' he muttered.

'Perhaps.' Larraby placed his hands on Judy's waist, and smiled drily. 'She isn't wearing anything tight, just take off her shoes.' He raised one eyelid, and said: 'It isn't morphia, the pupil's fairly large.'

'We'll have to get a doctor.'

'I don't think that will be necessary,' Larraby hazarded. He felt her pulse. 'All she needs, in my opinion, is warmth and comfort, she'll come round when the drug's effect has worn off, and won't feel any ill-effects.'

'How can you be sure?' demanded Lionel, hotly. 'And who is going to look after her? Mrs. Mannering isn't here, and the maid——' He broke off.

'Was murdered,' Larraby finished for him. 'I think we should wait for a while before we make any decisions. Mr. Mannering may telephone us; he certainly will if he can. Don't get so worked up, Lionel.'

'*I'm* new to this kind of thing,' Lionel growled.

'But you gave me the impression you wanted to learn,' Larraby said. 'The one positive fact is that Mr. Mannering was in a desperate hurry to get back to Ellesmere Square or he would not have left the young lady with a taxi-driver. But he will also tell you that in such an emergency a taxi-driver will either do what he's asked or go to the police.' Larraby paused. 'Obviously he believes Miss Vandemeyer to be in grave danger or he would not have taken the chance of being caught with her. So, presumably she was drugged preparatory to being abducted. And there are already two people missing in this case: Lady Vandemeyer herself and the man Gillespie.

What conclusions do you draw from this?'

'We must hold on to her like grim death,' said Lionel stubbornly.

'You are most certainly right. I think perhaps we should arrange for a policewoman——'

He broke off, as the telephone bell rang, hesitated, and then went into the hall to answer it. Lionel stood in the doorway as Larraby announced quite calmly:

'This is Mr. Mannering's residence ... Who ... *Hallo,* Superintendent!' Relief spread over Larraby's face. 'Yes ... I am here with Mr. Spencer ... yes, that is right. I thought perhaps a policewoman or a nurse whom you can trust might stay here for the night ... I think she is likely to be unconscious for some hours still ... It would be wise, I'm sure ... No, sir, Mr. Mannering left no word, and I am a little uneasy about him ... Very good Superintendent.'

He rang off.

'Bristow will lay everything on and will be here in half-an-hour,' he announced. 'So there won't be any need to worry about Judy.'

Lionel said, frowning: 'There could be a lot of reasons to be worried about Mr. Mannering. What do you think I should do?'

'Consult the Superintendent,' said Larraby firmly. 'I don't have any doubt at all.'

'I'm not so sure,' Lionel said. 'There's another cause for anxiety, don't forget.'

'What, precisely?'

'Supposing that taxi-driver was followed.'

'*Most* unlikely,' declared Larraby. 'Mr. Mannering left her alone for several minutes in the taxi and if anyone had followed her, that would have been his chance to act.'

Lionel conceded almost grudgingly: 'I suppose you're

right. Everything's pretty well under control, isn't it?'
After a pause, he went on: 'I didn't realise that Mr.
Mannering worked so closely with the police.'

'There are a lot of things you don't realise about Mr.
Mannering,' Larraby said drily. 'I wish——'

The telephone bell rang again, and he broke off to go
to answer it. This time, there was no delight at all in his
expression as he demanded: 'Who is that?' He motioned
to another room and mouthed: 'Extension!' Lionel
opened a door, saw a telephone near it, and snatched up
a receiver, in time to hear a man saying:

'Never mind who I am. Just bring the girl.'

'I really have no idea what you mean,' Larraby stated.

'Then I'll tell you. A girl was taken away from Vandemeyer's house in Ellesmere Square tonight, and taken to
Mannering's place. It was a big mistake. If you don't
want to get hurt, you bring her right back.'

'You are talking nonsense,' Larry interrupted. 'Both
Mr. and Mrs. Mannering are out of town, and——'

'Bring her, you hear me!' growled the man on the
telephone. 'If you don't——'

There was a sudden explosive roar from the door, and
Lionel spun round, banging against a sideboard of
bottles. He could see smoke, the door splitting from its
hinges, and a man wearing a scarf over his face and carrying a gun, emerging like a dark-clad ghost. Larraby
dropped the receiver and jumped towards the door of the
girl's room.

The man who had broken in raised a gun.

There was a flash, the crack of the shot, and then a gasp
from Larraby, who pitched sprawling. As he fell, another
man, also masked and armed, appeared from the smoke.
To Lionel Spencer it all seemed like a nightmare, or
something seen in a film.

One man said: ' Where is she?'

'Soon find out,' growled the other.

'When you find her, kill her and get it over.'

'He said we were to take her back——'

'We wouldn't have a chance in hell of getting away with her. She's had it—the little bitch has caused us too much trouble already.'

Lionel was standing stock still.

Only the fact that he was standing on one side and there was no light on in the room saved him from being seen.

He could see Larraby, clutching his thigh; the smoke; the two men with their guns: and the open door of the room where Judy lay. There were three other doors, besides hers and this one.

One man approached the door of Judy's room, the other a door on the right.

Larraby was gasping: The words sounded like: 'Police, police.' The man nearest him gave a bark of a laugh, and said:

'The cops can't help you. We fixed them.'

Lionel could just make out the shape of the bottles he had nearly knocked over. He stretched out and gripped the neck of one of them, fearful of making a noise. He took another, and stepped into the doorway. The man near Judy's room kicked the door open with his foot.

Lionel flung one bottle with all his force at the back of the man's head. As he transferred the second bottle to his right hand, the man he had struck pitched forward, the other spun round, gun levelled. Lionel, knowing that he hadn't time to throw before the other fired, felt as if death were yawning before him.

Larraby shot out his right hand and snatched the man's ankle. The shot spat out, the man fell, Lionel flung himself forward bringing the bottle down on the falling man's head. Larraby, trying to crawl into the girl's room, muttered hoarsely:

'Others ... might be others.'

'God!' gasped Lionel.

He bent down and lifted Larraby beneath the arms and half-dragged, half-carried him into the room where Judy was lying. He placed Larraby clear of the door, then slammed it, and as he did so caught a glimpse of the man he had hit first, swinging towards him, gun in hand. He heard the shot. The bullet pecked into the door. He switched on the light, saw the key in the lock and turned it. Two more shots rang out before silence fell.

'Don't—don't try anything else,' pleaded Larraby. 'Don't play hero—once is enough.'

Lionel said: 'The devils. The murderous devils.' He glanced at Judy, who seemed to be fast asleep, then looked down and saw the blood seeping from Larraby's leg. He went down on one knee, the better to examine it.

Twenty minutes later, when Bristow arrived, he found his own men unconscious in the street, the door blown down, a man dead of a fractured skull in the hallway of the flat, Lionel Spencer in the bathroom, ringing out a towel, and the girl still unconscious. Larraby was on the floor, a pillow beneath his head, and the wound in the fleshy part of his thigh covered with a face cloth.

Almost at the same time, a police-surgeon arrived.

Bristow saw Larraby off in an ambulance, and was assured by the police doctor that Judy Vandemeyer was in a drugged sleep, he saw a Murder Squad busy in this hall for the second time in a week, and then took young Spencer into Mannering's drawing-room. Spencer's eyes held the satisfied look of a man who had seen action. He was badly dishevelled, but he seemed as cool as ice.

'If these men were prepared to kill Miss Vandemeyer, sir, it could only be because of what she could tell the police. And if they'll kill as cold-bloodedly as that, they'll cut Mr. Mannering's throat as lief as look at him. I think we should raid 17 Ellesmere Square at once.'

The policeman at the end of his career and the youth at the beginning of his, stood staring at each other.

'I shouldn't worry too much about that,' said Bristow. 'I've men in the Square, the house is even covered from a roof opposite. The question is, whether we'll help Mannering most by raiding the house or waiting for a few hours. I've known him do some remarkable things. And if we do raid, it will be no guarantee that they won't kill him.'

'You've got to raid it now,' growled Lionel. 'If you won't——'

'You will, is that it?' Bristow concealed a smile, as if he had taken a great liking to this young man. 'You can't risk it, Mr. Spencer. I won't let you.'

'For God's sake listen to me,' pleaded Lionel. 'He's in there—he might never get out alive. I must——' He broke off, and Bristow marvelled, for he had seen just such a change of expression in Mannering's face in the past when Mannering had thought of some almost desperate, always daring venture. 'I can go and demand to see Judy!' he cried. 'I can be the worried boy-friend, say she was to telephone me but didn't, and I insist on seeing her. That would distract them, wouldn't it? You could raid them while I'm shouting the odds.' He paused, and then went on tensely: 'You can't refuse that. It will give Mr. Mannering a chance—it may be his only one.'

Slowly, Bristow said: 'You may have something there. It might be a good idea.'

CHAPTER 15

THE SEARCH

MANNERING was stifling his laughter as the banging came at the passage door of his suite. The outburst was partly from reaction and relief, he knew: it was a long time since he had put so much into a burst of furious activity. Even young Lionel could not have worked at greater speed.

Now, he had to face the men outside; had to be in complete control of himself.

He got up from the arm of the chair, smoothed down his hair, called: 'I'm coming!' and then slipped into the bedroom, kicked off his shoes, slid his feet into slippers, and went back and opened the door.

Buff was there, with Wells just behind him. Buff had an ugly graze over his right eye, and his collar and tie were loose.

'What on earth——' began Mannering, and then stopped and stared as if amazed. 'What—what happened to your eye?' he demanded.

Buff said: 'Out of my way.' He pushed past, strode into the living-room and glared about him, swung round and strode towards the bedroom. Mannering put out a hand to stop him.

'Don't,' warned Wells.

Mannering gripped Buff by the arm, spun him round and pushed him into the passage, saw Wells move forward to attack, shaping as if he were a judo expert, thrust out his right leg and planted his foot in Wells's stomach and flung him staggering after Buff.

Mannering stood in the doorway, looking down. Some-one was hurrying up from the first landing, but Manner-ing watched these two closely, expecting one of them to pull out a weapon.

'Marriott! Buff! Wells!' It was Vandemeyer, calling out in a shrill, agitated voice. 'What's going on here?'

Mannering turned on him furiously: 'Your thugs attacked me, but I can take care of myself. If they try any more tricks I'll break their necks. Keep them away from me until I get out of this place. I need just half-an-hour.'

He swung round towards his rooms.

'Marriott!' cried Vandemeyer.

'I'm through,' Mannering rasped. 'I don't like being followed wherever I go, I don't like apes like Buff riding roughshod over me.' Mannering went into his bedroom and pulled a suitcase from the top of the wardrobe and flung it on the bed.

'Marriott, I'm sorry if you've been insulted,' Vande-meyer said pleadingly. 'But——'

'It's a waste of time talking,' Mannering said. 'I'm through.'

Vandemeyer might take him at his word and so undo what good had been done, but he had to force this issue, and he did not think Vandemeyer would want him to go. He yanked open a drawer in the dressing-table, as his employer came in.

'Marriott, I beg you to sleep on this,' he said. 'If you still want to go in the morning, then I'll accept your de-cision. But tonight all of us are very distressed.'

'*Distressed?* Buff behaved like a lunatic!'

'My daughter has run away,' Vandemeyer said, 'and it was Buff's duty to see that she didn't—you know how overwrought she's been. And——'

'Just having Buff around would make anyone over-wrought,' growled Mannering.

'Marriott, that attitude won't help——'

Mannering turned to face the other squarely. Buff and Wells were still in the passage, Buff with a handkerchief at his forehead, Wells expressionless.

'What makes you think I want to help?' Mannering demanded. 'I came here to do a job, not to be pushed around and spied on by your lackeys. You can get some-one else to do your cataloguing, I'm not hard up for a pound.'

He did not understand why Vandemeyer looked so desperate, and still less did he understand it when Buff came forward and spoke more pleasantly than he had yet done.

'Okay, Marriott, so I blew my top. I'm sorry. I can understand that a man doesn't want to be pushed around. I had to find out what you're made of. Okay, so I know. You could have helped Judy run away, I caught a glimpse of a guy and it could have been you. I had to check whether you were up in your rooms.'

'I've been up here all evening.'

'So I was wrong,' Buff said. 'So I've apologised.'

'Sleep on it, Marriott,' urged Vandemeyer.

'Oh, all right,' said Mannering. He saw relief on both men's faces, and his own tone and expression changed. 'I'm sorry about Judy, I thought she was much happier tonight.'

'So did I,' said Vandemeyer. 'She fooled me, I'm afraid. Did she give you any hint that she had friends who would help her?'

'She didn't seem to have any friends,' Mannering replied. 'I've told you all I know, sir ... Do you think she will be all right? Should you ask the police——'

'We don't want a scandal,' Vandemeyer said more sharply. 'I'll see you in the morning.'

'Very good.'

Buff said: 'You can certainly look after yourself, Marriott. Where did you learn?'

'In America,' answered Mannering off-handedly. 'A man who has to protect fortunes in jewels and *objets d'art* doesn't last long unless he knows the tricks.'

'You keep a gun?' asked Buff.

'Yes—*and* I'm not afraid to use it.'

'I guess you wouldn't be,' said Buff, almost admiringly. 'See you.'

He walked off.

'Goodnight, Marriott,' Vandemeyer said.

'Goodnight.' Mannering closed the door on them, wiped the sweat off his forehead, and went into the living-room. On the television, three men were sitting at a table, talking about humanism. He watched without listening, then turned the set off, made himself some coffee, and drank it while pondering what had happened to Judy. He had taken everything so much in his stride that only now was he able to assess the situation here.

The most significant thing was that they wanted Judy out of the way. Buff had demanded it, and Vandemeyer and the woman who either was, or was not, his wife had connived at it. They had expected her to rebel, had been ready with a hypodermic shot which had put the girl out almost instantaneously. She must know something which could be dangerous to them and, inevitably, would help Mannering.

Second in significance was Vandemeyer's anxiety to keep him, 'Marriott', here—and Buff's readiness to pacify him. The secret they shared must be of vital importance to them both.

What was the relationship between them?

Buff seemed to have the last word on most issues, and it could only be because he could bring pressure on Vandemeyer: could blackmail him. Was the switch in 'wives' the reason? Was Vandemeyer doing what he was told in order to protect his real wife?

At least that was possible; and it was equally possible that the secret lay in this house.

Would there be a better night to find out?

Buff had had a rough time and would soon be out on his feet. Vandemeyer was on the point of collapse. Wells and his wife slept in the back of the house and the secret wasn't likely to be found there. He, Mannering, knew the house well now, and did not think that any lock he had seen here would keep him out of a room. The burglar alarm system was to prevent anyone breaking in, and should offer him little threat. And if these things weren't enough, he was in the right mood. The need for swift action over Judy had broken through the inhibitions of the years, and he had climbed in and out of his room with as much agility as he would have shown ten years before.

He would have a couple of hours sleep, and then look round.

He undressed, was in bed by half-past eleven, and asleep in a few minutes, quite confident that he would wake by half-past one.

The illuminated dial of his bedside clock showed twenty minutes to two when he woke. He lay for a few moments, got up, and dressed in a dark suit. Then he draped a towel over his shoulders, sat in front of the bathroom mirror and began to remove his make-up. He worked with intense concentration, watching his real self gradually emerge. A spirit lotion took the colour out of his skin and hair, and loosened the gum off his eyes. He rubbed cold cream into his lips to smooth the lines. Half-an-hour after he had started, he was once again John Mannering of Quinns.

He put the make-up box into a plastic bag and placed it on top of the ledge above his window, where it was hidden by the guttering. Then he opened the passage door with extreme care.

No one was in sight.

He stepped close to the wall, to lessen the risk of creaking boards, and reached the landing; the only other room here was a box-room filled with trunks and suitcases. He had tried the handle before and found it unlocked; it was still unlocked.

He crept down the top flight of stairs, and no matter how close to the wall he trod, there were faint creaking sounds. Half way down he thought he heard a rustle of movement and he flattened himself against the wall, but no one appeared. Waiting a moment, he continued on, and reached the main landing.

He *did* hear movement!

He peered down the main staircase, and saw a man sitting in the passage, a torch shining on the leaves of a paperback book he was reading.

The man coughed, and glanced about him.

It would be impossible to have any freedom of movement while the guard was free. Mannering flattened himself against the wall again and went down crabwise. Except for the turning of a page and another cough, there was no sound.

Mannering slid his left hand into his pocket, and took out a box of matches. He tossed it to the door and it struck, lightly. The man jerked up, catching his breath. After a pause of two or three seconds he stood up, staring

at the door. One glance towards Mannering would mean
discovery but the guard was interested only in the door,
from which the noise had come.

Mannering held his breath until the guard was standing, back towards him. Then he took the blue scarf from
his neck, crept forward and dropped it over the other's
head, tightened it round the neck, and drew it fiercely
tight. The torch dropped to the floor. The man fell
backwards against him, clutched at the scarf but could
not loosen it. The only sounds were those of a man chok-
ing.

They faded at last.

Mannering let him go, carefully, picked up the torch,
then half-carried and half-dragged him along the passage.
Opposite the anteroom was a door beneath the stairs, and
it was not locked. Mannering opened it, and shone the
torch inside. There were fuse boxes and a single switch.
He pressed it, and light filled the cellar staircase.
Manoeuvring the man down these, Mannering laid him
out on the cement floor, and felt for his pulse.

He was alive.

Mannering went farther into the cellar, finding three
rooms, one of them a carpenter's workshop. A ball of thick
string stood on a bench and Mannering cut off two
lengths, bound his victim's wrists and ankles, and then
used his own handkerchief as a gag. The man's eyes
flickered open.

'Don't try to escape or you'll really get hurt,' Mannering said in his normal voice.

He looked about the cellar.

In one alcove was the oil burner for the central heat-
ing, in another several small packing cases and dozens of
picture frames, in the third household oddments—from
camp beds and mattresses to pieces of carpet and odd

chairs. There was an old-fashioned coal chute which hadn't been used for a long time and shone with white paint. A faint pattern of light showed through the circular grating at street level. Two iron staples had been driven into the chute beneath the grating, to prevent anyone from getting in from the street, but the grating itself was loose.

There was no time to do anything there now.

Mannering went back, passing the prisoner who was rolling his eyes and trying to mouth words. Mannering checked the cord, loosened the gag a little, and went up to the ground floor. He closed the cellar door and stood poised for a moment. Then he entered the dining-room.

It was beautifully but plainly furnished with a Sheraton dining-table and twelve chairs. There was a sideboard, and this Mannering checked; quick measurements with a steel tape showed that there was no room for concealed hiding-places. He checked the alcoves and the big archway which led to the kitchen, and came to the conclusion that this room held no secrets.

He went into the farther, and by comparison, smaller room in which he had met the others earlier in the evening. He calculated that it was directly beneath Vandemeyer's study. There was a corner cabinet here, too, directly beneath the movable one upstairs—though this one was filled with rare pieces of china and porcelain. Nearby was a writing-desk, and Mannering recalled that Vandemeyer had moved his right hand to the side of his desk upstairs, before moving the cabinet. Mannering went to the desk, sat at it, and felt cautiously along the side. There seemed to be nothing. He tried again, seeing beneath the overlapping top of the table a tiny spot slightly above the surface level.

He pressed—and felt it move. When he ran his fingers

over the surface again, he could feel nothing.

He crossed to the cabinet and touching approximately the same spot that Vandemeyer had touched in the cabinet upstairs when he wanted to get into the treasure house. Again he felt a slight protuberance, and pressed.

The cabinet swung back from the wall in exactly the same way as the other.

Could this lead to yet another treasure house?

He felt sure that the button in the desk broke the alarm circuit; if he had attempted to operate the cabinet by itself the alarm would have been raised. There was danger that there would be another alarm circuit, and to make an escape route he placed a heavy chair between the back of the cabinet and the wall; he could not be shut in.

Now he used the torch.

It shone on shallow steps and a passage, exactly as the one above, but these walls were bare. A blank wall faced him. He had to find the control button for this before he could go farther on, and scanned the roof.

A tiny indentation virtually invited him to press it. But this could be the second alarm and he looked for something less obvious. He seemed to be there for an age before he saw a paper-thin slit between wall and ceiling.

He took out his pen-knife, opened a blade, and inserted it gently; he felt resistance which soon gave way, and the wall which barred his progress slid slowly to one side. Ahead was a heavy velvet curtain. He pulled this aside very carefully, and as he did so, lights came on ahead, exactly as they had done upstairs.

This chamber was wider and the shelves and alcoves were deeper. On them were articles of unbelievable splendour, and after his first gasp of astonishment, he looked more closely, realising that each was beyond price.

Here were the crowns of princes and of dukes; here were bejewelled swords and breastplates, daggers and caskets; here were treasures from the near and the far East, from this age and from all the ages of history. This collection surpassed the one upstairs in a way Mannering would never have imagined possible.

There was another kind of difference, too.

Vandemeyer could not have come by them honestly. Mannering had never seen, nor even dreamed of a hoard of stolen jewels of such incalculable value.

And at the end of this chamber there was another wall.

CHAPTER 16

THE TUNNEL

MANNERING, dazed by what he had seen, began to ask himself whether he should call this a day and go back, or whether he should try to find what lay ahead. He went back into the room and heard no sound but the sonorous boom of a striking clock chiming three.

This was the hour when most people slept soundly.

He went back, heart in mouth, forcing himself to pass the *objets* on each side, although he could have lingered over each, and told the history of many. One of them made him stop in his tracks: a jewelled turban known as the Crown of Ghengis Khan, ablaze with the colours of every jewel known to man. He passed on, seeking the secret of the sliding wall ahead, yet telling himself there might not be one, there must be an end to these treasures.

And these were stolen, he reminded himself: some had been missing for twenty years or more.

He saw a faint groove in the ceiling, noticeable only when he stood in a certain spot. There were no cracks, no protuberances. He stretched up and pressed and immediately the wall in front of him slid open.

This did not lead to another treasure house; instead there was a passage which was little more than a tunnel. Walls and ceiling were rough plastered like the floor which sloped downwards, but there were no shelves and no alcoves. Here and there the walls widened and there were some packing cases, corrugated paper, wrapping paper and thick string. He paused to judge his position, and realised that where he stood was underneath the porch of Number 17, and that this tunnel ran across the road, beneath the garden and—he needed no telling—to the house across the square. There was a subdued light from the ceiling, just enough to see by. He went slowly, counting each pace. He had counted seventy-one when he reached a shallow flight of steps. There was a door at the top of them.

He went up and tried the handle; the door was locked.
Or was it bolted?

No, he reasoned—it would have to be approached from either side, a bolt would prohibit this. He took his knife from his pocket and opened it to a blade which looked-like a long needle but in fact was a skeleton key. The key-hole was large and of the old-fashioned mortice lock; it should not be difficult to pick.

He felt the instrument catch, turned cautiously, felt pressure yielding—and then the lock clicked back.

The sound was very loud, louder in this confined space than anything he had yet heard. Was it as noticeable on the other side? He kept quite still but heard nothing, turned the handle again, and pulled.

The door yielded, slowly, squeaking faintly.

There was no light beyond.

All he must do here was find where the doorway led, and the size of the cellar of this house; it would be folly to stay longer, equal folly not to learn as much as he could. Cautiously he flicked on his torch. He was stand-ing in the middle of a cellar about the size of the car-penter's shop beneath Number 17 Ellesmere Square.

And in a corner, on a camp bed, lay a man.

The man seemed to be asleep, for he did not stir, gave no indication that he had been disturbed. Bedclothes were thrown loosely over him, one bare foot stuck out at the end of the bed. As Mannering drew nearer he saw a head of sparse white hair, and a pale wizened face. Nearer still, he saw that the frail left hand had a steel bracelet which was fastened to the bare brick wall by a black chain.

This must be Gillespie; who else could it be?

Was he alive and drugged to coma?

Or was he dead?

Mannering drew close to the emaciated figure, hatred welling up in him for the men who had done this thing. The man's lined face bristled with stubble of at least a week's growth. Mannering gritted his teeth as he slipped a hand between the filthy shirt and the skin stretched tight over prominent ribs.

Why do *this* to any man?

Mannering found the heart and felt it beating firmly; so the prisoner was not dead, but drugged. He drew back, facing the alternatives—to free this man and take him away now, or to get away and send for the police.

If he tried to carry the prisoner, it might take too long for safety. And he had to close all the entrances, to make sure that no one noticed the forced entry. Yet if he went off alone, this man might die, or, if the guard in the other cellar was found, be taken away, before help could reach him.

The sensible thing was to go back, alone, and telephone Scotland Yard. There was no question now of keeping anything from the police; what he had discovered in the secret treasure house was all the evidence they would need to investigate Vandemeyer's activities. Why this had happened, what pressure Buff was exerting on Vandemeyer, why there was a substitute wife—all these things would be discovered one by one.

He must take Gillespie away if it were possible.

If it *was* Gillespie.

Who else would it be? he asked himself again.

He placed the torch on the side of the bed so that the beam shone fully on to the bracelet and the chain. There were swellings and sores round the wrist—God, what a fiendish way to treat a human being.

The 'bracelet' was an old iron ring which hinged open, and was kept in position by a lock, and such a lock was difficult to force. Mannering's skeleton key was not small enough; what he really needed was a file. He had a file blade in his knife but it would take an age to get through this. He examined the ring in the wall. It had been cemented in and the only way to free it would be to chip away the cement. Sawing or chipping would be heard.

They had made quite sure that Gillespie couldn't escape.

Mannering was an expert on locks and keys, and knew that it would take twenty minutes to force this one. He could be back in the house and on the telephone in five.

He hated leaving the prisoner here, but there was no choice.

He replaced the blankets, and turned away. Not once during the whole period had Gillespie shown the slightest indication that he knew anything was going on, and he still did not stir.

Mannering went back along the tunnel, hurrying, yet careful not to make too much noise. When he reached the farther steps he had a moment's fear that the doors might be closed against him, but the first one was open and the blaze of light reflected from the stolen treasures was dazzling. He passed through into the second chamber and into the anteroom.

The room was exactly as he had left it, and there was no sound. There was a telephone there, but if he lifted it, a ringing then in another part of the house might wake Buff or Wells. He hesitated, heart thumping. He was still sickened by what he had found and the fierce excitement at the discovery of the second treasure house had gone completely.

He had to risk disturbing others, now. He——

He heard a sound, on the staircase.

He stood stock still for a moment and then moved to the wall alongside the door. The noise was repeated, unmistakable, furtive. Someone was coming down the stairs. He heard the sound of agitated breathing and thought it more like a woman's than a man's.

Suddenly, as he peered through the opening between door and wall to see who it was, bright light flashed on.

A woman screamed on a muted note.

A man—Buff—called in a vicious voice: 'Going places, my lady?'

'Deirdre' Vandemeyer gasped: 'No, I—no! I couldn't sleep, I——'

'So you put on a coat to have a walk round the house,' sneered Buff. 'Turn around and come back.'

'I—*you* can't order me about!' She almost screeched the words.

'Can't I?' sneered Buff. 'I'll try again—turn around and come right back.'

'No! No, I refuse!'

'You'll wish you'd obeyed me, my lady. I've had as much as I can take tonight, I'd be glad to take it out on somebody.'

'I—I'll scream the house down!'

'And who's going to hear you? Your so-called husband couldn't wake if a bomb dropped on him, Wells couldn't care less, none of the others can hear you.'

'*Mr. Marriott would!*' she gasped.

'Up on the top floor he couldn't hear you if you screamed your heart out. Do what I tell you, or——'

She shrieked wildly: 'No, no!' Suddenly she moved and rushed down the stairs, passing his door, flinging herself at the front door. A chain clattered, there were other noises as she tried to open the door. Mannering kept absolutely still; at all costs he must not reveal himself at this juncture.

The uncanny thing was Buff's silence and his slow, deliberate movements.

The woman was clawing at the lock, which must have a patent fitment which she didn't know how to open. Buff passed Mannering. He had a gun in his left hand, and his right was held in front of him, reminding Mannering vividly of his stance just before he had attacked Judy. There was a curl at his lips which showed just a glimpse of his teeth. He looked more animal than human.

'No!' the woman choked. 'Don't come any nearer, don't come!' She was half-sobbing and near hysteria. '*Keep away from me.*'

Buff was now between Mannering and the front door, and Mannering stepped into the passage. The woman did not notice him, all her attention was focused on the man who menaced her. She had stopped trying to open the door and had her back to it, pressing desperately as if she thought it would open by magic.

Mannering took two long strides, gripped Buff by the arms and spun him round and then hit him with all his strength on the point of the chin. Buff rose up a little on his toes; for the second time that night Mannering saw his eyes roll as he toppled backwards. His head thumped the floor only a few inches from the woman's feet.

She stood quite still, absolutely petrified.

'It's all right,' Mannering said in his normal speaking voice. 'He can't hurt you now.'

She opened her mouth but only gasped for breath.

'You can relax,' Mannering reassured her. 'No one's going to hurt you, now. You'll be all right.'

'Who—who are you?'

Her voice was high and uneven, and he knew that he must handle her very carefully if he were not to have a hysterical woman on his hands.

'I'm a friend of Gillespie,' he said.

'Gillespie!' she echoed.

'I've come to look for him,' said Mannering. 'I'm glad I was in time to help you.' He looked down at Buff, and asked: 'Who is that?'

'He—he works for my husband, he——' She caught her breath again. '*How did you get in?*'

'Through a window,' Mannering answered easily. 'Do relax, Lady Vandemeyer. There's nothing at all to worry about now. The quicker we tell the police——'

He saw on the instant that he had made a mistake by saying 'police'. He did not know why he had said what he had—unless it was because he so desperately wanted to bring them here and that for a moment his defences were down. He went on almost without a pause.

'. . . this man can be charged with assault, there's nothing at all to worry about.'

'No,' she said, in a sighing voice. 'I can't——'

Mannering saw her glance down at Buff. He must be extremely careful, a moment's carelessness over Buff could lead to utter disaster. He felt very tired from reaction, wanted just a few minutes in which he had nothing to think about, and he moved in a sudden burst of action, bending down and picking the man up by his coat collar, dragging him to the cloakroom by the front door. He knew the tiny window, knew that it was barred. He pushed Buff between the W.C. pedestal and the wall, then withdrew into the hall and slammed and locked the door.

The woman was still by the front door, but now she had a pistol in her right hand, and was covering him. Her hand wasn't steady, but at such a range it was impossible for anyone to miss.

'You're not going to call the police,' she said. 'I won't let you.'

She was still very pale, but the desperation of terror had gone; she knew exactly what she was doing and had herself under firm control. Mannering stared at her almost stupidly, the gun had taken him utterly by surprise. A question flashed through his mind: Why hadn't she used the gun on Buff? But it was a pointless question, and he had another much more pressing one to answer.

What was he going to do?

At least there was no danger from Buff or—presumably —from Vandemeyer. If Wells or any of the other staff were going to appear at all they would surely have appeared by now. So there was only 'Deirdre' to handle and the best way would probably be to humour her.

'Do you hear me?' she demanded. 'You're not going to send for the police.'

'Well, you've got a point,' he said wryly. 'I never argue with a gun.'

'And you'd better not argue with me!'

'I certainly won't. Why don't you want the police here, though?'

'This—this is a personal affair.'

'I see. It didn't look very personal just now. May I remind you that you would have had a very rough time if

I hadn't stopped your friend.'

'You can remind me but you're not going to send for the police!'

'So you said,' said Mannering. 'And now that I've had time to reflect, I don't want them any more than you do.'

She flashed: 'What do you mean?'

'I've no right here,' he pointed out. 'I broke in to try to find out what had happened to Gillespie. Do you know?' he asked suddenly.

'No!' she cried. 'I've no idea!'

'I was only asking,' Mannering said ruefully. 'I am what the police call a burglar, since I broke in. It would be difficult to prove that I didn't come to steal, so——' He shrugged. 'What are you going to do? Will your husband be able to cope when he does wake up?'

After a short pause, she said: '*I* can cope.'

'With the brute I locked in there?'

'No,' she said. 'With *you*. If you'll help me, if you'll do exactly what I tell you I'll let you go free, and I'll pay you well, I'll pay you a fortune!' Eagerness blazed in her eyes. 'Do you agree? Make up your mind—will you do exactly what I tell you?'

CHAPTER 17

WOMAN PROPOSES

FOR the first time Mannering realised that she was really beautiful. Flushed with excitement and hope, young and vital, she looked a different woman. Her eyes were a peculiar shade of porcelain blue, those eyes which had first made Lorna suspicious. She was breathing hard, her lips slightly parted.

'I'll do what you tell me if you make it worth my while,' Mannering said.

'Oh. I'll make it worth——' She broke off. 'You'll do what I tell you whether I make it worth your while or not.'

Mannering said: 'Let's not argue. What do you want me to do?'

'If you are a friend of Gillespie's, it's more than likely that you're an expert on jewels and works of art. Are you?'

'As it happens, I know quite a bit about them.'

'Well, then, I'll tell you. There's a fortune in this house!'

'So I've heard.'

'It's *mine*.'

'I thought it was your husband's.'

'It's *mine*. Jewels like those are for a woman, not for an old man to gloat over.' She drew nearer, the gun still pointing at him, and he did not like the way her hand shook. 'They all think I'm a fool, just a stooge, but they're wrong. *I've* got the brains.'

'I don't need telling that,' Mannering said glibly.

'I knew they'd never get away with what they're planing to do, so *I* made plans to get away. I've a passage ooked to Paris, tomorrow. I wasn't going to stay here, nyhow, only long enough to get—to get my share.'

'*Very* clever,' Mannering approved, straight-faced.

'I'm a damned sight cleverer than you!'

'I'm not arguing,' Mannering said. 'How much time do e have?'

'Time? *Time!*' Her eyes blazed. 'We haven't long, we've ot to get a move on! You must do exactly what I tell ou. Do you understand?'

'I will, when you tell me.'

'There's a tunnel under the Square,' she cried.

'A *tunnel?*' Mannering sounded astonished.

'It leads across to the house on the other side of the quare, he owns that too. He owns most of the houses ere, and people who work for him live in them. If he ants them he just rings for them.'

'I see,' Mannering said. 'But he can't ring now, can he?'

'He's dead to the world,' 'Deirdre' declared. 'He can't leep until he's made himself stupid with dope. He's the ast man to worry about.'

'And Buff's the last man, too.'

'Yes, but there are plenty of others. Don't make any aistake, there are plenty of others, and they—they won't esitate to kill.'

'Who *are* they?' asked Mannering much more lightly han he felt.

'It doesn't matter! The—they're Buff's men. We nustn't let them come here.'

'Stop them coming through the tunnel, you mean?'

'Yes.'

'How?'

'Blow it up!' she cried. 'I told you I was clever. I've some dynamite, I stole it from Buff's room when I first had the idea. There's enough to blow the tunnel up, no one can possibly get through.'

'And then?'

'We'll take his jewels,' 'Deirdre' said triumphantly. 'We'll pack them in suitcases and take them away. There must be millions of pounds worth.'

'Oh, there are,' agreed Mannering.

She wasn't normal, of course; first the wild impulsive attempt to escape by the front door, and now this theatrical, Guy Fawkes plot to blow up the tunnel. He had the impression that she was living under a stimulant—that she had taken a drug to pep up her courage. She did not really know what she was doing or saying. She was jumpy and unpredictable, and he would have to be very careful indeed. If he crossed her she would probably shoot him. As things were and for as long as she believed he was doing what he told her, she would keep on boasting and talking, and letting cats out of the bag.

He wanted to know the whole truth.

And he wanted to find the real Deirdre Vandemeyer.

'We ought to get a move on,' he said again.

'*I'm* not stopping you. Can you get into the study?'

'Not—not without the keys,' he lied.

'*I've* got the keys to the study door. Do you know the corner cupboard? Can you open it?' Words spilled from the woman's lips.

'I think so.'

'You'd better be sure,' 'Deirdre' said. 'You lead the way. And don't forget I'm just behind you with the gun.'

He went ahead, knowing that with a single movement he could kick the gun out of her hand. There was a risk that she would press the trigger and shoot him, but that risk didn't keep him back. He had to find out all she knew.

He reached the landing, and the study door.

'What about Wells and the other servants?' he asked.

'They can't hear from this part of the house, and they're off duty. Stand aside—and don't think I won't shoot you.' He moved as he was told, and she took a key from a pocket in her skirt. The muzzle of the gun made patterns in the air, he was on edge lest it go off by accident.

The door opened.

'You go in first,' she insisted. 'Go on. Hurry!'

He went in and crossed immediately to the corner cupboard. She watched him groping much more than he needed to; it would not be wise to find the way into the Treasure House too easily. He was thinking that there must be a way from this floor to the tunnel but he hadn't yet found it. Suddenly he muttered to himself:

'He does something at the desk before he opens this.' He strode past her, making no attempt to get the gun, hoping to convince her that she had nothing to fear from him. He reached the desk and began to press from a position in Vandemeyer's chair.

'For God's sake hurry!' she screeched.

'I'm being as quick as I can.'

'You're like a snail. Here, let me——'

'I've found it!' exclaimed Mannering. 'Didn't you hear that click?' He jumped up and passed her again, reached the corner cupboard and pressed the side, and the cupboard began to move away from the wall.

'It's opening!' she cried. 'It's opening!'

'Yes, I can see it is.'

'Stand back! You're in the way!'

He moved a foot, watching the door and the hole in

the floor appear. Her eyes glistened and she moistened her lips in an almost lascivious way.

Very slowly and deliberately, Mannering asked: 'Do you know where the real Lady Vandemeyer is?'

She hardly reacted at first, obviously not taking the question in. Then she jumped round and thrust the gun closer to him, eyes blazing with anger. His heart began to thump.

'What the hell do you mean? *I'm* Lady Vandemeyer.'

'Don't be absurd,' Mannering said. 'I came to get some of these jewels but I couldn't get them on my own. You can't get them without help, either. If you were the McCoy you wouldn't have to take them this way.'

'You—*know* that?'

'Yes. Where is she?'

'It doesn't matter where she is,' 'Deirdre' said harshly.

'I want to know.'

'If you don't get a move on you'll never know anything again!'

Mannering stood in the entrance to the Treasure House and spoke with flat finality.

'I want to know if she's dead. If she is, it's a murder rap, and I don't intend to——'

'She's not dead! He wouldn't let them kill her, wouldn't——'

'Who is "he"?'

'Vandemeyer, of course!'

'Who wanted to kill his wife?' asked Mannering quietly.

'*They* did. *Buff* did! She knew too much——' She broke off and screamed at him: 'Stop asking these questions. Go ahead—go *on*!'

She gestured with the pistol, and Mannering shrugged as if with resignation, and went into the first chamber.

With the gun in his back, the knowledge of all that had happened, the dangers and the fears, he was still swept to astonishment at the scintillating radiance about him. He glanced over his shoulder and saw the woman open-mouthed in wonder, as if stupefied by the sight of so much jewellery, so much beauty, so much wealth.

The gun dropped towards the floor.

Mannering simply turned round, as if marvelling, and took the gun from her. She was so affected by all she saw that at first she didn't try to stop him. Then she realised what he was doing, tried to snatch it back and when she could not, flung herself at him.

Mannering was carried almost off his balance by the fury of her onslaught. He grabbed a shelf, sending diamond rings and brooches flying in cascades of radiance to the floor. She clawed at his eyes, at the same time bringing her knee up towards his groin. He twisted his body and took the blow on his thigh. Her mouth wide open, she was screaming on an uncanny, stifled note, as if she had some measure of control despite the unbridled fury of the attack.

Suddenly, instead of backing away, he went forward. Their bodies collided, the force of the impact proving the furious intensity of her attack. She tried to draw back but he flung his arms round her and held her, vice-like, against him. He could feel the thump of her heart as she strained to get away. Then she lowered her head, to butt him in the face, but he dodged in time and simply raised a hand to the back of her head, and crushed her to him.

She began to gasp for breath.

She was up to any trick, he knew.

She began to pant, and her body went limp, her eyes closed, her head lolled to one side. Very slowly and carefully Mannering eased his hold—and in a flash she was writhing and kicking again, and the toe of her shoe caught him on the shin.

He winced with pain, and anger suddenly took over.

He spun her round, pulled her arms behind her, holding her wrists in one hand. He took the blue scarf from his neck and used it as a rope to tie her hands behind her, and only then did he let her go.

She staggered against the shelves, and priceless jewels fell to the floor like pebbles.

He dabbed at his lacerated face, conscious, too, of his abraded shin. He moved back a pace in case she decided to kick out again—and as he went out of reach, she did.

On the same instant there was a thump of sound beneath them.

'What's that? *What was it?*' she gasped.

There was another thump, almost immediately beneath them.

'Someone's coming!' she informed him mechanically. 'Someone's heard us!'

Mannering took her gun from his pocket, and spoke for the first time since her onslaught.

'If they have, blame yourself.' He moved farther away so that he could watch both her and the opening into the study, ears strained to catch any sound of footsteps. There was none, but bumping and thumping went on below.

'It's not in the house, it's in the tunnel!' she said, whispering. 'It's beneath us.'

'I think you're right,' agreed Mannering. He went to the opening and peered about the study; the room was empty and the house seemed silent. 'Deirdre' did not launch another attack, her fears had transferred to the threat down below. As he looked back at her, Mannering was caught by her beauty again; fear and rage had given life to her expression, put fire into her eyes.

'What—what are we going to do?' she asked huskily.

'I know what I ought to do,' said Mannering harshly.

'What do you mean?'

'I ought to take the jewels and run, locking you in here until the police find you.'

'Oh no!' she gasped. 'Oh, dear God, please don't do that.'

'Keep your voice down!'

'I—I'm sorry, I lost my head. But don't—don't leave me. You can have *half* the jewels, take any you like but don't leave me here.' She moved towards him and asked as if in a wondering voice: 'Did *I* do that to your face?'

'You did.'

'I'm sorry, I really am. Please don't leave——'

'Listen to me,' Mannering said, still harshly. 'I'll let you go with half of this if you'll answer a few questions.'

'But there's no time. *Listen!* Men are moving about downstairs, they'll soon come up. We've got to hurry.'

'We don't move from here until you answer my questions.'

'*Then ask them, you fool!*' she screeched, deep in her throat.

'Who are you?' Mannering demanded.

'I—I'm Lily Davies. I—I'm an actress. I've known Buff for years. Years.'

'Did he make you stand in for Lady Vandemeyer?'

'Yes,' she said, and words spilled out of her. 'He said there was a chance in a million. I had to stand in as Vandy's wife. I said it was crazy but he said Vandy would go along with it—and the old creep did! It was all laid on. Lady Vandemeyer went away, *I* came back in her place. I'm very like her, that's why Buff thought of me, I didn't need to do much, just make up a bit older, that was all. They changed all the servants, no one here could have spotted the change except old Gillespie and Judy— and Judy was supposed to be in France, she was going with a party of friends but some of them caught chicken-pox or something and she came back. *She* knew I wasn't her stepmother but Vandy persuaded her not to talk about it. I don't know any more, I swear I don't—*we've got to go*. Hark at those men downstairs.'

'I can hear,' Mannering said.

'They're hammering something!'

'I can hear that too. What happened to Gillespie?'

'*He* knew something was wrong—his sight was failing, he couldn't see me properly, but he knew from my voice. He told Vandy he knew Buff was blackmailing him, begged Vandy to go to the police. And he and Judy hatched up some plot which Buff found out.'

'What happened to him?' Mannering demanded remorsely.

'They took him away! I don't know any more. They didn't let me know much but I saw these jewels once. Buff said I'd get as many as I could cram into my biggest handbag when it was all over.'

'What did you have to do to help?' demanded Mannering.

'Just—just pretend to be Vandemeyer's wife. Just put on the act, that's all.'

'But *why*?'

'I tell you I don't know!' The woman was at screaming point.

'Is Buff blackmailing Vandemeyer?'

'I don't know what you'd call it. He can twist Vandy round his little finger, there were times when I was almost sorry for the little squirt. Buff's got something on him all right but don't ask me what, he——'

She broke off and caught her breath, her eyes rounded with astonishment. She was facing the opening that led to Vandemeyer's study. Mannering thought on the instant that she was trying to make him believe someone else was coming, but he glanced round as she screeched: 'It's closing!'

And the wall *was* closing up. The corner cabinet was swinging into position. Mannering made a wild leap forward, but as he touched the back of the cabinet it clocked into place.

And the lights went out.

Lionel Spencer pulled up outside 17 Ellesmere Square, switched off the engine, and jumped out. His movements were quick and decisive; he was breathing a little faster than usual, that was all.

A light shone brightly on the white paint of the porch.

He rang the bell, drew back a pace, and forced himself not to look round. It was some reassurance that police were on the roof and at each entrance to the Square, but Larraby had been shot so cold-bloodedly, he was prepared for anything to happen almost before he could think.

No one came. He pressed again, with the same result; then rat-tat-tatted on the brass knocker, the hard metallic sound echoing all about the Square. As the echoes faded footsteps sounded behind him. He turned, to see Superintendent Bristow and two police officers.

'There's no answer at all,' Lionel said, puzzled. 'They can't have flown, can they?'

'We'll have a look,' Bristow said. 'Get in through the window or break down a door,' he ordered his men.

Ten minutes later, they had been through every room

in the house. Upstairs there were signs of hurried packing; downstairs, there was no sign of haste at all. No one was in any of the rooms—but in the cloak-room by the front door were frayed ends of cord, suggesting that a man had been tied up there, and cut free.

Bristow himself opened the door to the cellar, and in the dim light from behind him he saw a man lying bound and gagged, with his head crushed in.

For a dreadful moment he thought it was Mannering.

For the same agonising moment, Lionel Spencer thought so too.

Then in a tone of indescribable relief, Bristow said: 'It's not Mannering.'

'Thank God for that,' Lionel breathed. 'But—where *is* he? He wouldn't have gone with the others willingly—he couldn't have!'

'Knowing John Mannering, I'd believe him capable of anything,' said Bristow.

CHAPTER 18

THE WALLS

MANNERING stood absolutely still in the pitch darkness. He could hear Lily breathing agitatedly, but that was the only sound, for the hammering below had stopped. It seemed an age before she said huskily:

'We—we're buried alive.'

'Nonsense,' Mannering said.

'We—we *are*!'

'They'll open up again soon.'

'You—you're only saying that.' There was a rustle of movement before she went on: 'I'm terrified.'

'Take it easy,' Mannering said soothingly. 'It is frightening, I know. Stay where you are a minute.'

'I—I want to be near you.'

'I won't run away,' Mannering said drily. 'I've a torch.'

'A torch—a *light*! Oh, thank God!'

He took a slim pencil torch from his pocket and a thin beam of intense white light cut like a dagger through the darkness. There was a rumbling noise below, but nothing like as loud as before. Mannering twisted the top of the torch and the light became diffused, spreading much farther but not dazzling. Lily had come only a little nearer, and he remembered almost with a shock that her hands were still tied behind her back. She looked unbelievably handsome, had a certain magnificence with her shoulders back and her figure like a statue.

'Lily,' Mannering said, 'will you promise not to play any tricks if I untie you?'

'Tricks?' she echoed. 'I'm too terrified to try anything.'

'You'd better be, because I would have to get rough if you did.'

'I—I won't be silly,' she said. 'I—I'd be a raving lunatic if I were here by myself. I've never needed a man around so much!'

Mannering laughed, in spite of himself. He went nearer, saying: 'Turn round.' He untied the scarf, still not absolutely sure that she would not attack him again, but all she did was to rub her hands and wrists, making a little slithering noise.

'How—how long will that torch last?'

'Two or three hours,' he answered.

'Sup—supposing they don't come back?' She was close to him, now.

'They will.'

'You can't possibly tell!'

'Use your head,' urged Mannering. 'How much are these jewels worth?'

She ejaculated: 'Of course!'

'The question is, how long will the others be?' Mannering went on as he placed the torch carefully on a shelf, resting it between a diamond and sapphire bracelet and a ruby corsage pin—each worth tens of thousands of pounds.

'Can—can you do anything?'

'I'm thinking as fast as I can,' he told her. 'Keep quiet for a bit, while I concentrate.'

She was staring at him intently, and he wondered what was passing through her mind. While there was the chance that he could help her she was unlikely to lose her self-control again. Later if the situation seemed to get worse, she might go berserk.

'Can—can we sit down?' she asked suddenly. 'My legs are aching.'

'Good idea,' agreed Mannering.

She slumped down, her limbs falling almost unconsciously into a pose of studied allure. 'Do you think I can smoke?'

He lowered himself rather stiffly beside her.

'It will be much better if you didn't.'

'So you do expect to be here a long time?'

'I think we might be, so why use up what air we've got.'

'You're right,' she said. She put her head on his shoulder. 'Go on, then. Concentrate.'

He leaned back against the wall, and brought all his concentration to bear on the situation. There was a fortune here, but a far greater one down in the other chambers, worth ten, twenty, thirty times as much. Vandemeyer or Buff might well decide to sacrifice these treasures, if there was sufficient risk to themselves in coming back for them.'

No one else knew of this store-house, so the only hope was for Buff or his men to come back for the jewels.

Hope, thought Mannering, almost desperately. What hope would there be of being left alive?

He pushed this fear to the back of his mind, wondering whether Buff had been released. And what about Vandemeyer and his drugged sleep?

There were many things still unknown, but their significance faded into the background. The only thing of vital importance was to find a way out of here. His thoughts veered towards what he knew of the control system. The first switch was at Vandemeyer's desk, the second at the corner cabinet. If the switch itself was in the desk there was no chance; if it was in the side of the cabinet he might conceivably get at it, if he could make a hole in the wall.

He needed an explosive, such as—dynamite! My God! Lily had come prepared to blow up the tunnel!

'Lily,' he said, hoarsely.

'Hm—hm?' She turned her head to look at him, surprisingly relaxed. Perhaps the outburst had drawn all the energy out of her, leaving her subdued and lethargic.

'How do you get into the tunnel?' Mannering asked.

'There's an entrance from the dining-room.'

'Dining-room?'

'Yes—the fireplace moves out, like the cabinet in the study. You go down a few steps and then a door opens into the tunnel.'

'What's in the tunnel?' asked Mannering.

'Nothing much—a few packing cases and boxes and some string and corrugated paper.'

'Nothing else?'

'What else would you expect?'

'No windows, for instance,' he improvised, but he was thinking that she would have been oblivious of everything except the treasures, had she known of them. The fireplace in the dining-room was on the same wall as the corner cupboard in the anteroom but at least forty feet away. So there were two entrances to the tunnel, one for easy passage to and from the dining-room, one through the house of stolen treasures. It was reasonable, and the obvious thing to do. It was equally obvious to have a way from this floor into the tunnel—down a few steps beyond the end cross wall, for instance.

'What are you thinking?' Lily demanded more urgently.

'Quiet a minute,' he urged.

There were no noises from below, now, but Lily was

sure that the tunnel was the one with packing cases and
other packing materials. It was easy to guess what the
noises were. The stolen treasures were being packed
away, and would be removed from here. Packing and re-
moving them would take hours—and a big van, even a
pantechnicon might be needed.

There could be no major removal until morning, that
was almost certain.

'Tell me,' Lily said, sharply. 'I'll explode in a minute!'

'Explode is exactly right,' he said. 'The problem is—
where?'

'Explode——' She broke off with a gasp. 'The dynamite!'

'Where is it?'

'In—in my bag.' She clutched her shoulder-bag tightly.
'But we'd blow ourselves up!'

'If we blow a hole near the tunnel Buff and his men
will be waiting for us,' said Mannering. 'So—it has to be
here.' He looked towards the spot where the corner cupboard turned this into a prison. 'Let's get up, and let me
have the dynamite.'

'I'm not going to let you blow us up!'

'Don't be silly,' Mannering said. 'I don't want to die
any more than you do.'

'Oh,' she said doubtfully, 'I suppose not.' She stood up
quickly, then opened her bag and placed two sticks of
dynamite in his hand, the red cases bright and new. They
stood facing each other for a moment, and she asked:
'Who are you?'

'Listen to me,' he said. 'There is another chamber
along there.' He pointed. 'And there is a sliding partition
in the wall which I think will still operate.' He groped
near the wall and then pressed, and slowly the partition
wall began to slide away.

'There it is!' cried Lily.

'Yes. Now if we blow a hole in *that* wall'—he pointed back to the cabinet—'while we're lying on our faces in that chamber'—he pointed towards the second chamber filled with *objets d'art* of such great value—'we won't get hurt. And there will be a good chance of getting at the mechanism of the corner cabinet. But the blast would smash half the contents of——'

'We can't worry about those now!' Her voice began to rise. 'It would be madness.'

'It will take ten minutes to shift them so that they should miss most of the blast,' Mannering said. 'And I'll need twenty to make a hole in the wall to put the dynamite in.'

After a pause, Lily said: 'I'll move the things, then.'

'Yes—down on to the bottom beneath the door,' urged Mannering.

He prised off the top of one stick of dynamite. Lily watched, and was still standing and staring when he started to chip away the wall. It was of cement, not plaster, and his strongest blade had little effect. He kept scraping and probing—and hearing Lily putting the *objets* on the bottom shelves. She was behaving remarkably well, but he still feared she might switch into a violent mood without warning.

Suddenly, he came upon sand and soil, and soon made a hole several inches deep. A pile of powdered cement and sand was on the floor by his feet, and there was a powdering over his hands and sleeves.

Lily appeared by his side, and asked sharply:

'Can't you hurry up?'

'No,' Mannering said, patiently. 'But by the time you've finished I'll be ready.'

He heard Lily breathing heavily. Suddenly she exclaimed: 'I've done it! Are you ready?' She came hurrying. 'You said you would be ready.'

'Let me have the rest of the dynamite.' He took the stick from her and began to push the powder inside the hole he had made, packing it tighter. Soon, he judged it full enough, he stuffed a corner of a handkerchief into the hole, leaving the rest of it hanging in a lightly twisted tail. It could fail, but there was a good chance that the explosion would break enough of the concrete away for him to get at the switch which controlled the corner cabinet.

'We'll soon find out if it will work,' he said. 'You go back and lie face downwards, about a foot from the wall.'

'You'll—you'll come, won't you?' It was a plea.

'As soon as I've lit the fuse,' he promised.

'Is—is there much danger?'

'There's some, but not very much.'

'I know,' she said. 'You don't want to die any more than I do.' She gave a hysterical little laugh. 'If anyone had told me I could have lived through today I would have called them daft.'

'You're wasting time,' Mannering reminded her.

She went away from him, and he bent down over the improvised fuse. There was absolutely no way of being sure what the effect of the blast might be, but there was nothing to do but take the risk. He glanced round. Lily was doing just what he told her. He struck a match, and held it to the tail of the handkerchief. It caught alight, the flame running more quickly than he had expected. He turned and scrambled back, forcing Lily to the ground, shielding her as far as possible.

The explosion came almost on the instant. There was a fierce crackle of sound, then a roar that was more like a thunder clap, a blast of air which rocked his body, then a clattering of things fell off the shelves and cement fell from the wall. He smelt the acrid stench of the explosive and when he opened his eyes they stung badly, and he could hardly see for smoke and dust. He rolled to one side, coughing, and Lily also began to cough. She sat up slowly, tears streaming down her face, as Mannering struggled to his feet.

Had he bared the switch?

It had been only a fifty-fifty chance. He groped his way towards the cabinet wall, could not see clearly but saw that a lot of the cement was cracked and pieces were chipped out.

Then he heard Buff call: 'That's as far as you go.'

Buff was at the other wall, by Lily's side, covering him with a revolver. With his left hand, he thrust Lily's arm up behind her, so that she could not move.

CHAPTER 19

THE REMOVAL MEN

THE sickness of disappointment was like nausea. From near triumph there was almost inevitable disaster. Mannering could not be sure even that he would live another minute, the hate in Buff's eyes was so unmistakable. Was it an hour ago or two hours since he had attacked the man? It didn't matter. The graze on his forehead had swollen and become bluish and ugly. His coat was torn, and there was a scratch on his cheek near the corner of his mouth—as if he, too, had been scratched with a pointed finger-nail.

He said: 'Who the hell *are* you? You're not Marriott. You——' He broke off, his voice rising in astonishment. 'My God, you're *Mannering*!'

'That's right,' said Mannering quietly. 'You made your biggest mistake when you tried to kill my wife.'

Buff gave a snort of laughter.

'So you're the great *Mannering*. If that ain't funny! I'll say this for you, you've come a lot farther than I ever thought you would.'

The sense of imminent disaster seemed to be lifting slightly, but Mannering wasn't fooled; that gun was unwavering in Buff's hand.

'Was the guy who saw Judy your assistant?' Buff demanded.

'Yes,' answered Mannering.

'You certainly made progress,' Buff admitted. He laughed again. 'You want to live?'

Mannering's heart leapt in sudden hope, sure that the question was meant seriously; it might not be a chance he could take but it gave him time, eased the tension still more; he even relaxed physically and leaned back against the shelves.

'Yes,' he said, 'I want to live.'

'Buff, let me go,' Lily begged suddenly. 'I didn't mean to——' Her words broke into an ear-splitting scream. '*You'll break my arm!*'

'Give me time and I'll break every bone in your body.' He eased his grip and pushed her, sending her sprawling to the floor, and her right hand swept along the shelf where she had stacked the *objets d'art* for safety. For the first time since the explosion, Mannering thought of them.

'So you want to live,' Buff said to Mannering.

'You can put it that way.'

'You've half a chance.'

'Tell me about it.'

'It won't take long. You've got quite a reputation at Quinns. You could be a front for me.'

'Front?' echoed Mannering.

'I've got a lot of art treasures for sale,' Buff said. 'I could keep you in business for life.'

'The stolen ones?' asked Mannering, and then feared he had made a mistake, for Buff's expression changed, his body seemed to stiffen.

'Have you seen them?' he demanded.

It was pointless to lie, so Mannering admitted:

'I've seen them.'

'If Vandemeyer showed you——' began Buff savagely.

'No one showed me,' Mannering said flatly.

'You couldn't have found——'

'Supposing you stop fooling yourself,' said Mannering,

his voice steady enough to hide his jumpy nerves. 'I found them on my own. What are you suggesting?'

'*Who showed them to you?*' rasped Buff. 'Did she?' He glared at Lily.

'I don't know what you're talking about,' she gasped. 'I swear I don't know.'

'That had better be true.' Buff looked very ugly. 'I don't believe Mannering could have got into this place by himself and I don't know anyone but you who would help him.'

'So you don't, don't you?' said Mannering, in the voice he had used in his guise of Marriott. 'See how much you don't know, Buff.'

'My God!' gasped Buff. 'You're Marriott too.' He caught his breath. 'But—but you don't look——' His voice trailed off in blank amazement. It was a moment when Mannering could have taken a chance and gone for him, but he did not think the chance was good enough. Buff recovered quickly, and raised the gun a fraction. 'How long do you think it would take you to sell those things?' he demanded.

Mannering considered, and then said: 'Five years at least.'

'Yes,' said Buff. 'That's about right, if you'd said much less I would have known you were lying. How would you do it?'

'I would choose the buyers singly, and with care,' Mannering answered.

'Buyers who would know they couldn't tell the world what they had?'

'Buyers who would know they were stolen,' Mannering replied evenly.

'So *Quinns* buys and sells hot goods.'

'I know who would be prepared to buy and could

afford to. I don't buy and sell stolen goods at Quinns. I never have.'

'Say you never will and I'll put a bullet through you,' rasped Buff.

'I would to save my life,' said Mannering simply.

'And the first chance you got, you'd turn me in,' Buff sneered. 'There's just one thing would make you do what I told you. The same thing that worked with Vandemeyer.' Mannering felt a chill run through his whole body as he saw the implication, but he showed no sign. 'You got your wife out of the way quick as light, didn't you. You want to know what would bring her back quicker than she went?' Mannering felt as if his blood were freezing but he still showed no sign. 'If she thought you were in trouble—and by God, you're in trouble!'

Mannering said flatly: 'You're wasting your time, Buff. She might risk her life but she wouldn't save hers or mine by turning Quinns into a crooked business.'

'She wouldn't?' Buff laughed on a shrill note. 'You don't know much about your wife, do you? When you've done what I want you to do at Quinns you can stop worrying about your better half. I——'

He broke off, at a sound from behind him. A man was approaching, and Mannering saw first his head and shoulders, then his body, as he came up the stairs. He was wearing a white carpenter's apron and a piece of green baize over the front.

'Can you spare a minute?' he asked.

'Who needs me?' Buff didn't look round but kept Mannering covered.

'We can't get that big case out of the tunnel without breaking a corner off the wall.'

'We got it in.'

'That was before the wall was plastered.'

'Okay,' said Buff. 'I'll come and see.' He motioned to Mannering and said to the man: 'Pick up Lily and don't be careful with her. Mannering, you go ahead and don't try any of your favourite tricks.' He squeezed to one side to allow Mannering to pass and followed close behind. At the top of the steps Mannering saw four or five men stacking boxes and small crates against the tunnel wall.

These were removal men, and they were packing the treasures from the lower chamber before taking them away. The tunnel was well lighted, and at the far end a big box stood with hardly an inch to spare on either side. 'You don't have to ask me what to do with that,' Buff said. 'Unpack it and use two smaller boxes.' He let the man who was carrying Lily squeeze past, she hung like a sack over his shoulder, and Mannering saw her right leg flex as she was almost level with Buff, and knew exactly what she was going to do. Buff, preoccupied with the box problem, didn't realise the danger until it was too late.

She kicked him with her pointed shoe and caught him on the mouth.

He let out a scream of agony, swayed and dropped his revolver. Mannering was after it before it reached the ground, snatched it up, and rasped:

'Let her go!'

The removal man, off balance because Lily had kicked out with such strength, staggered. Before he had recovered, Lily slid off his shoulder and gave him so violent a push that he toppled down the stairs. The other men along the passage swung round, staring towards the steps. Buff was on his knees, his face in his hands.

'Keep still, all of you!' Mannering called. 'I'll shoot the first man who moves.'

There was a moment of absolute stillness, until two men at the far end of the tunnel dropped what they were holding and ran towards the steps that led into the house across the Square. Mannering knew that he could not stop them. But if he fired he might scare the others.

Then Vandemeyer appeared at the far steps, and he also carried a gun.

'That's enough,' he said in a clear, carrying voice. 'It's all over. I've found my wife.'

That was the moment when Bristow and Lionel Spencer saw a man who was working on the cabinet in the corner of the study, put out his left hand and give the thumbs up signal. He stood back and pulled at the cabinet, which began to move away from the wall. Beyond was an opening and a short flight of steps, dim light and floating clouds of dust.

A voice sounded clearly from a long way off.

'I've found my wife.'

'*My wife—wife—wife——*' echoed and re-echoed.

Bristow hardly heard it. He was looking at the jewels scattered over the floor, on the shelves, in the alcoves, some of them mixed up with pieces of cement and wood—a carpet of dirt and rubble mixed with gems which glowed and shone in a hundred different hues.

'*Mr. Mannering!*' called Lionel in a tone of deep relief. 'Mr. Mannering, thank God you're safe.'

Mannering heard him less clearly than he heard Vandemeyer.

He was a foot or two away from the crouching Buff, who hadn't moved since he had fallen. There was an uncanny silence for several seconds, before Mannering called out:

'What did you say, Vandemeyer?'

'I've found my wife. They had kept her prisoner, I——

Good God, it's *Mannering*!'

'That's right,' said Mannering. 'Have you also found Gillespie?'

'I've found his body,' Vandemeyer said. 'They starved him to death. He—— *Mannering*!' he screamed. 'Look out, Buff——'

Buff was springing to his feet. There was a wild look in his eyes, but he had no weapon, there was nothing he could do but leap at Mannering. And as he did so, Vandemeyer shot him from behind. The bullet struck him in the head and he pitched forward with only a grunt of sound.

Lionel Spencer and several policemen were rushing from one direction. Vandemeyer approached slowly from the other, and the 'removal men' were herded together in the middle. Bristow gripped Mannering's shoulder, then bent down to examine Buff—although there was little need. Yard officers went along and handcuffed the men who did not give even a token resistance. Lily was leaning against the wall, shivering from reaction. Vandemeyer reached Mannering, and said quietly. 'I don't know how you became involved, Mannering, but thank God you did. The first thing I must do is get a doctor—I think my wife is all right, but I must be sure.'

'Where is she?' Mannering asked gruffly.

'In a room in a house across the Square. She is in a drugged sleep, but they seem to have treated her well.' He closed his eyes and stood motionless for a moment. 'It's been—unbearable. They kidnapped her, and then forced me to do what they wanted so as to save her life. They forced me to keep a vast hoard of stolen jewels here, they forced me to buy and sell piece after piece. And I had to, Mannering, I had to, if I wanted to save my wife's life.'

He looked very, very old.

He began to move forward, slowly.

'We can talk later, can't we?' he pleaded. 'I must tele-phone——'

'Lionel, go with Sir Cornelius,' Mannering said. 'Do whatever he asks, and stand by. And I *mean* stand by.'

'I will, sir,' promised Lionel. 'I—oh, lord! I'd forgotten.' He stood in sudden alarm and his expression was such that he struck a knife of fear into Mannering. 'I—I hate to say it, sir, but Josh Larraby's been shot. He's at the St. Stephen's Hospital in the Fulham Road.'

Mannering asked roughly: 'How badly is he hurt?'

'Not too badly, I understand, sir.'

'All right,' said Mannering. 'You carry on.' He was gritting his teeth as he turned away, after a glimpse of Vandemeyer's bowed shoulders and Lionel striding after him. In the other direction, the police were herding the prisoners together and Bristow was looking down at the litter of precious things.

'Bill——' began Mannering.

'Unbelievable,' said Bristow. 'Utterly unbelievable. There must be—millions upon millions of jewels here. I mean, *pounds*worth of jewels. And surely that—that diamond and emerald crown is the Maharajah of Kanab's. Surely——'

'Yes, it is,' said Mannering. 'I've never seen a collection like this, Bill—and every piece was stolen. You're going out in a blaze of glory. Do something for me, will you?'

'Of course,' Bristow replied.

'Come with me to see Gillespie's body, and to see Lady Vandemeyer before Vandemeyer comes back,' said Mannering. As he drew level with Lily, who was leaning against the wall with someone's whisky flask in her hand, he went on: 'And let Lily Davies turn Queen's Evidence.

I think it's time she had a break.'

Lily gave a mirthless little laugh.

'Thank heavens I didn't shoot you,' she said.

Mannering led the way along the tunnel. On the bed, still chained to the wall, was Gillespie. There was no doubt at all that he was dead. Bristow's expression hardened when he saw the emaciated face and the sores at the chained wrist. A plainclothes man came hurrying along, and as he drew up, he said:

'I've a key for that damned ring, sir.'

'Get him free,' said Bristow.

'But don't move him until a doctor's seen him,' Mannering pleaded. 'I have a feeling he was suffocated, not simply left to die.' He was thinking that had things worked out differently he might have saved Gillespie's life, but he made no comment, and nor did Bristow.

They found more men in the house across the Square, which was now in the hands of the police; and they found the real Deirdre Vandemeyer in an attic room at the top of the house. It was plainly but comfortably furnished. Nothing suggested that she had been ill-treated, but she was drugged to the point of coma.

'So Vandemeyer was blackmailed by the threat to his wife's life,' Bristow said. 'I've never ceased to wonder what a man will do for a woman. Or a woman for a man for that matter.'

'Nor a wealthy man for the treasures of the earth,' Mannering said grimly. 'Bill, listen to me . . .'

As he talked, he looked down on Deirdre Vandemeyer who was so calm in sleep, so lovely. And as he looked at her, her face seemed to fade and Lorna's to replace it.

Lorna, who was now in no danger but who, because of this sleeping beauty had come so near to death.

CHAPTER 20

THE WICKED ONE

A FULL eight hours sleep had done Cornelius Vandemeyer a world of good. The years seemed to have rolled off him, his eyes were bright, his movements brisk as he led the way into his study. A cupboard from another room had replaced the damaged one. Behind the walls the police were searching with rare diligence for the scattered gems. Other police, with help from the British Museum, the Victoria and Albert Museum, Christies and Sothebys, were cataloguing the rediscovered stolen goods. With them were several experts from those insurance companies most likely to be affected.

The morning newspapers had been too late for the story; the London evenings carried a little, but within an hour or so new hordes of newspapermen would flood this house, the Yard and Quinns with questions.

'First things first,' said Vandemeyer, as the others sat down. 'You say that Judy is quite unhurt, Mannering.'

'Yes, and well-cared for.'

'I am—well, needless to say I couldn't be more glad. Or grateful. I'm sure you know that.' Vandemeyer picked up three sheets of paper, filled with typewriting, and handled them with a curious kind of fastidious care. 'Now, Superintendent, you will require a statement, I suppose by way of a confession from me. I have typed it out. Would you like me to read it, or give you the salient points?'

'Let's have the salient points,' said Bristow.

'Very well. You need no telling of the background—my own love of and collection of precious stones, miniatures and *objets d'art*. I make no secret of it—I made my millions and invested in these treasures. My love for them developed gradually. Sometimes I overstretched myself but my wife, wealthy in her own right, came to my rescue. I had this house converted and the chambers built underground to protect my possessions. And I bought other property in Ellesmere Square and let it.

'One of my tenants was a man named Buff.'

Vandemeyer paused, but neither of the others spoke, so he went on:

'I knew that Buff let off rooms and small apartments—a common practice in this neighbourhood. So it did not surprise me that a lot of different men went in and out of the house opposite. Buff paid the rent regularly and so far as I knew was a good tenant. What I didn't know was that he was a very clever thief and buyer of stolen jewels, and that he was tunnelling towards my tunnel.'

Vandemeyer drew a deep breath and looked extremely distressed.

'I learned long afterwards, that he had bribed my old and as I thought most faithful servant, Gillespie, to give him the information. Gillespie was in my full confidence; he even knew how far my secret chambers extended. It was a very simple matter for him to tunnel through until only a few inches of earth separated the two places.

'Then, Buff brought his secret hoard of stolen gems and *objets d'art* to the tunnel,' went on Vandemeyer, 'and he was ready to put his major plan into operation. He wanted me to buy the stolen jewels or to put them on the market. Of course I refused—I would not listen.

'But I *had* to listen, gentlemen, when he threatened to harm my wife. He knew what you will now know to be

true, that there was no law I would not break, no sacrifice
I would not make, for the safety of my wife. I needed one
absolute assurance: that she would live with me in comfort, would be free from all fears and dangers.

'Buff undertook to ensure these things, and for a long
while, did so without question.

'Gradually, however, his demands on me and on my
one confidant, Gillespie, grew more excessive, more difficult to carry out. I had not known of the enormous hoard
of stolen treasures kept in my property—I knew of some,
not of all. Buff, obviously fearful that he would be suspected by others, perhaps by the police, whom he had so
long deceived and in fact derided'—Vandemeyer looked
levelly at Bristow—'demanded that I should *buy* any
of his stolen hoard that I could not sell. It was impossible.
I told him so. As a result—he kidnapped my wife.'

Vandemeyer's voice seemed to fade into silence, and he
leaned back in his chair, closing his eyes. It was a long
time before he spoke again, and then it was hesitantly
and huskily.

'Buff had planned this for a long time. When the moment came to act, he put on tremendous pressure in order
to make the quickest possible killing. He created a reign
of terror, threatening Judy, threatening me—and yet
keeping my hopes alive by promising not to kill my wife,
simply to make a getaway. Once the police investigated,
after he had gone, they would know *I* was not to
blame.

'He had trained a woman who was like my wife in
outward appearance, to impersonate her. To the outside
world, all was to appear normal, otherwise I could not
sell for him or buy from him. He knew that I could not
go on for very long, that sooner or later I would give way.
Our servants were dismissed, some who had been with the

family for years. Every precaution was taken but'—Vandemeyer drew in a hissing breath, as if seized by sudden pain—'Gillespie became concerned and knew that I was being blackmailed. He thought the only way to help me was to fight Buff, and he threatened to go to the police. He was locked away in the tunnel—kept alive only because of his knowledge of certain of the treasures, their value, and who might be persuaded to buy them. And my daughter came home unexpectedly and realised at once that the woman now established as her stepmother, was in fact another person. For a few days she and Gillespie worked together, and after he disappeared she was frantic. *Frantic!* But'—again the old man's voice broke—'she listened to my pleading, my assurance that this nightmare life would not go on for ever.

'Then something happened—a chance encounter between your wife, Mannering, and the woman who was impersonating mine.

'I can tell you this. When at first I agreed that your wife should paint Deirdre's portrait, I had some vague thought of asking your help. I knew of your great reputation, your extensive knowledge of the market and your trade connections. But Buff insisted that all the sittings for the portrait be here—where he could have all the conversations with your wife recorded, and so I dare not give her even a hint. I did not know—I beg you to believe that I did not know—that he planned your wife's murder. I knew of nothing until afterwards, when it became obvious that things were coming to a dreadful climax.

'But he held my wife captive and threatened such dreadful things. And he had at his command so many men, all thieves and hardened criminals, many of them vicious and brutal.

'I was too afraid to fight. To my eternal shame, I was too afraid.'

Vandemeyer's voice died away into a sighing whisper of sound, and for a long time there was silence. There was no movement in the room nor any they could hear outside it, until the old man picked up the sheets of typewritten paper and they quivered in his hand.

'Vandemeyer,' Mannering said, 'will you answer me one question?'

'If I can—yes, of course.'

'When did you first begin to buy stolen jewels, and begin your unique collection?'

Vandemeyer started violently.

'*What* did you say?'

'When did you first buy stolen jewels——'

'But that is not true! I had all the money I wanted, I had no need——'

'Vandemeyer,' interrupted Mannering, 'Buff didn't suddenly acquire such power over you, and you would never have made such sacrifices for your wife.'

'Mannering! What a thing for you, of all people, to deny! Your wife is everything to you, she——'

'Gillespie and your wife were beginning to know too much,' Mannering said, quietly. 'And for years Buff must have been carrying out daring thefts and bringing the stolen goods to you. He had all the men, experts at safe-breaking, at picking and blowing locks. Some of the goods in your strong-room were stolen twenty years ago, and a man like Buff wouldn't have hoarded that kind of fortune for twenty years. When did your partnership begin? You, the buyer: Buff, the man who knew that whatever he stole, you would buy.'

'Superintendent!' cried Vandemeyer, 'this is utterly nonsensical!'

'I hope so,' Bristow said heavily.

'You must not listen——'

'The police will listen and soon a judge and jury will listen,' said Mannering. 'When did it begin—and when did you and Buff fall out? What really happened? Did you decide to pay him off, or even to kill him? Did you want to rid yourself of the past—and did Buff then show his hand? Is that why you killed him last night?'

'But he was going to kill you!'

'Nonsense. I was in no danger, and you know it. Is that why you finally killed Gillespie, too—to make sure he could never tell the truth?'

'Oh, God, this is dreadful—dreadful!' gasped Vandemeyer. 'There is not a word of truth in it. What malice has got into you, Mannering, to invent such wicked charges?'

'Not malice,' Mannering said evenly. 'Facts. First, Lily Davies told me that you talk in your sleep—so presumably you slept with her, which means you weren't quite so distraught as you made out about your wife. Second, you took me on, as Marriott, and let me know the secrets of your strong-room; I didn't believe you would take such a chance with a stranger unless you planned to kill him when he had done what you wanted, which, in this case, was to check everything Buff had done with your treasures, making sure there were no fakes. You said that Buff suddenly started buying stolen jewels, but you could be using him as a cover, rather than Buff using you. So many things didn't square with you being the victim. And if I had any doubts they vanished when I found a tape-recorder attached to your bed—*he* was anxious to know what *you* were planning. Doubtless when all was over, you meant to kill him as well, and put all the blame on his shoulders.' Mannering took a tiny tape-recorder from his pocket and placed it on the desk. 'This was built into the head-board, would you like to hear——?'

Vandemeyer snatched up the recorder, sprang to his feet and stood glaring, as if he did not know what to do.

'Sir Cornelius Vandemeyer,' Bristow said formally, 'I must ask you to come with me to Scotland Yard to answer certain questions.'

Two hours later, Mannering, Judy, Lionel Spencer and Brian Rennie were gathered in the office at Quinns, when the telephone rang. Mannering had just finished relating the story of what had happened, and Judy was sitting almost limp with distress.

'Yes,' said Mannering. 'Yes, Bill.' He saw the others tense as they realised the caller was Bristow. 'Yes? . . . *Full* confession? . . . Yes, I'm very glad. . . It will make it easier for everyone . . . I'm sure she will, you can reassure him completely.'

Mannering put down the receiver, and looked at Judy.

'Judy,' he said. 'He wants you to go and see your step-mother, and try to help her. Will you go right away?'

'Of course!' Judy sprang up, eager to have something to do.

'May I take you to Ellesmere Square?' asked Lionel, quickly.

'Oh, *please*—and may Lionel stay for a while, Mr. Mannering?'

'For as long as you need him,' Mannering told her.

He went with them to the door, and watched them drive off. He felt tired and in no way elated, but was glad at least that there would be some comfort for Deirdre, and her stepdaughter. As he went into the office, Rennie

as answering the telephone, and he held the receiver
ut to Mannering.

'Thanks. Who? ... Josh! Am I glad to hear you.'
Mannering sounded delighted.

'And I to hear you, sir. I have a telephone next to my
ed, and can keep in touch with everything that goes on
.. The doctors say I will be walking in ten days or so.
Would you mind telling me what has happened.'

Mannering told him, in most lucid outline.

'May I offer my deep congratulations, sir,' said Lar-
aby.

'Thanks, Josh, but they're not due to me ... All right,
'll believe you! ... Take it easy, I've a suspicion that we
hall be asked to sort out the collections and value them
n today's market, there's no peace for the wicked.' He
aughed again and then rang off.

'He must be nearly eighty, and he can't wait to get
back to work,' he said.

'A remarkable man,' remarked Rennie, with feeling.
'Nearly as remarkable as you, John.' He paused. 'So you'll
ave the job of sorting all this out, dealing with owners
nd the insurance companies and salerooms. I can't think
of a better man for the job. John——'

'Yes,' Mannering said mildly.

'Will you forgive me if I renege on my offer?'

Mannering's smile broadened, and he shook his head.

'It's a fabulous business,' went on Rennie, 'but it's too
isky for me, and no one could ever take your place. And
rom what Josh has told me, this kind of thing has been
going on for over twenty years. It's part of Quinns. I just
ouldn't stand it, and I know my wife wouldn't stand for
t.'

'And mine certainly wouldn't blame her,' said Manner-
ng. 'Are you going to fly back to New York?'

'Tomorrow, if that's all right with you.'

'Of course,' said Mannering. 'Will you tell Lorna just what's happened and assure her that there's no danger now—and that before too long I think she will be able to finish the portrait.'

'I'll be delighted to,' said Rennie.

When he had gone, Mannering was alone in his office. Lionel wouldn't be back today, and Judy needed him as much as her stepmother needed Judy. A very promising young man, the most promising he had ever employed. There was still a lot of energy left in Josh Larraby who would want to work until he dropped, but Mannering needed help and the enthusiasm of youth. With the old man and the young, he could make a good team.

But not a big enough team.

A thought which had entered his head fleetingly a few days ago, came back. Bill Bristow was soon to retire. If he felt like helping part-time at Quinns...

'Nonsense!' exclaimed Mannering aloud. 'It's impossible!'

But the idea did not leave him again, and he began to hope, if not to think, that it might become a reality.

Another book in the BARON series

THE BARON AND
THE MISSING OLD MASTERS

When John Mannering went to value an old lady's paintings, deep in the heart of Wiltshire, he walked straight into a hornet's nest—hornets that blackmailed, burned and murdered. They blackmailed a beautiful young girl, who almost paid for her silence with her life, they burned down houses to destroy the evidence of their crimes, and they tried—several times—to kill John Mannering. And then it became a battle for the truth. Who was blackmailing whom? Why? Joanna's silence seemed to make her suspect; but his instincts told the Baron that what she was hiding was not guilt, but honesty.

Other Books in the Series:

All these books are available at your bookshop or newsagent or can be ordered direct from the publisher. Just tick the titles you want and fill in the form below.

....

CORONET BOOKS, Cash Sales Department, P.O. Box 11, Falmouth, Cornwall.

Please send cheque or postal order, not money, and allow 7p per book (6p per book on orders of five copies and over) to cover the cost of postage and packing in U.K., 7p per copy overseas.

Name..

Address..

....